MW01142711

ETERNAL WILLOW

A NOVEL BY AMBER RAINEY

Blue Forge Press
Port Orchard ❦ Washington

Eternal Willow
Copyright 2017
by Amber Rainey

First eBook Edition
October 2017

First Print Edition
October 2017

Second Print Edition
May 2019

Cover art by Erik Rainey
Cover design by Brianne DiMarco
Interior design by Brianne DiMarco

All rights reserved, including the right to reproduce this
book or portions thereof in any form whatsoever, except in
the case of short excerpts for use in reviews of the book.

For information about film, reprint or other subsidiary
rights, contact: blueforgepress@gmail.com

This is a work of fiction. Names, characters, locations, and
all other story elements are the product of the authors'
imaginations and are used fictitiously. Any resemblance to
actual persons, living or dead, or other elements in real life,
is purely coincidental.

Blue Forge Press
7419 Ebbert Drive Southeast
Port Orchard, Washington 98367
360.550.2071 ph.txt

DEDICATION

To Erik, who always believes in me. I love you.

Acknowledgements

There are so many people that make a novel possible and many don't realize that without them, it would not have happened.

First, thank you, Erik. You are the one who puts up with the roller coaster of my emotions the most. You coax me out from under the covers when I try to hide away from myself and my thoughts of inadequacy. You consistently believe in me and, whether I show it or not, your support is instrumental to my success.

Thank you, Kellan, for allowing me to be your mommy and for teaching me something new every day.

Thank you, Maria Fowler, for being my editor. Every character in this book is better because you questioned my intentions with each one of them and you were not afraid to tell me what you truly thought each step of the way. You allowed me to blossom as a writer.

Thank you, Giennie, for allowing me to bounce my initial ideas off you and for always being a sounding board when I need it. You are a perpetual cheerleader in my corner!

Thank you, Staci, for reading it and telling me how much you loved the book but also how mad you were at me. I knew I had done my job well, even if I broke your heart.

Thank you, Jennifer and Brianne and everyone at Blue Forge Press. You guys are some of the best people to have in your corner and I am very blessed to have met you.

Last but certainly not least, thank you Allen O'Donoghue for your infinite wisdom and patience. You have been a rock for me for many years, my friend. It is your faith in me that often keeps me going. Without you, I would never have ventured so far outside of my initial comfort zone and my confidence in myself has grown by leaps and bounds. Words will never describe the impact you have had in my life. I am a stronger person thanks to your tireless efforts!

Amber Rainey

ETERNAL WILLOW

A NOVEL BY AMBER RAINEY

PROLOGUE

Now

The long branches of the willow tree swayed in the breeze and skimmed the water of the lake, light ripples created by the green leaves forming ever-increasing concentric patterns across the surface. A few ducks swam along the edges, occasionally dipping their heads under the surface and coming up with breakfast as they flapped their wings to reset them from being under water. The tall grasses, once so full of flowers, now grew wild in the early autumn sun. Dawn was but a few hours past and Ciarán relished the serenity of this quiet place where he had spent so much of his youth. He idly rubbed his hand over a spot in the tree's trunk where long ago he had carved the letters OC in an intertwining pattern. He coughed lightly and sat down, the trek from the castle not a long one but still winding him. Leaning his head against the trunk, he took in a huge breath and slowly let it out, stifling the next cough that threatened to burst out at the sudden intrusion of air on his sore throat.

He would be headed back home soon, and Ciarán felt a sense of foreboding that this would be the last time he would have a moment in this spot. This tree had witnessed so many happy memories and, if he were honest, it had seen its fair share of sorrow as well. He looked over at the little memorial near the tree and rubbed his hand over it. Yes, the tree was witness to all. Its long branches hid its secrets from the world. Theirs, too.

He spotted Kellan standing awkwardly at the edge of the tree's perimeter, two guards standing further back in the field. Ciarán moved to get up and Kellan quickly sought to prevent the gesture.

"No need. May I sit?" Kellan asked.

Ciarán chuckled. "Of course, it is your land."

"Aye, but it was once your home as well." Kellan caressed the tree trunk; his magic had always been in tune with nature. "This tree seems to remember you more than me. I think it misses Orla as well."

He studied Ciarán for a moment as the latter coughed. His lifelong friend was not well and doing a poor job of covering it up.

"Do you still plan on returning to Fadersogn today?"

"Aye, Your Majesty. I promised to return and with no offense to your hospitality, I miss my own bed." Ciarán bowed his head a little at the admission.

"She would understand if I sent word that you were unwell, my friend. A few more days rest might do wonders for your health."

Ciarán thought for a moment and then lightly ribbed, "You and I both know that she would bring every doctor in Fadersogn riding winged horses if she could manage it."

Kellan laughed at that. Indeed, his sister would not take kindly to him keeping her Captain occupied for more than the allotted time. She had already sent at least two messengers asking about their progress and if the business might be completed earlier than previously discussed.

"Also, you of all people should know I am no longer allowed the luxury of delay. Not since..." His words trailed and he paused, taking a breath. "It is best I return as scheduled," Ciarán finished lightly.

Kellan nodded. "Yes. Will you tell her?"

Ciarán looked away and thought for a moment. He sighed deeply and shook his head. "Not yet. It would pain her too much and she would blame herself. Or worse, she would blame Olav and Lochlann would haunt me for the days I have left."

Both men sat under the tree in comfortable silence for a long moment, the stillness occasionally broken by a duck quacking or the periodic coughs from Ciarán. Finally, Kellan rose and Ciarán followed him.

"You are most welcome to return at any time, with or without her blessing. We miss your company." Kellan clasped Ciarán's shoulder.

Ciarán bowed. "Thank you, Your Majesty. I do enjoy seeing you and hope that we might enjoy a visit from you as well. Your niece and nephews are always delighted at your magical antics."

"Enough of that 'majesty' nonsense. Best be off before the day gets too long."

"Aye," Ciarán agreed.

They walked through the weeds of the meadow and joined back up with the guards, slowly making their way into the castle grounds where Ciarán's traveling group waited for him. Ciarán checked his saddlebags, then mounted his horse.

"May the road rise to meet you, Ciarán." Kellan's heart was heavy with worry for his friend, but he kept his voice light.

"Kellan, may you enjoy peace and prosperity." Ciarán waved and headed out the gates.

Kellan sighed, watching Ciarán fade into the distance as he rode away. "And may the Gods grant Orla the strength for what is to come."

chapter one

Queen Orla of Fadersogn loved her children more than anything in the world. She delighted in the uniqueness of each child. She enjoyed spending time with them, both individually and as a family. Erik, at almost twenty, was the oldest and—with his dark red hair and green eyes—he looked the most like his mother. He was the rightful heir to his father and would one day be king of the land. Runa was a beautiful girl of seventeen with blonde hair the color of late afternoon sun. She was a perfect blend of both her parents, though she inherited much of her mother's personality, for better or worse. Quinn, barely fourteen years old, had jet black hair and eyes the color of forget-me-nots. He was the youngest, and the one who still shadowed his mother the most. He was also the only one of her children who had inherited her magical abilities and therefore received extra instruction from her.

Orla beamed as their father, King Olav, taught them

how to sail tiny boats in the garden fountains. All too soon, her children would venture out into the world and have lives and families of their own. However, today they were together and even Erik, who had deemed himself too old for childish pursuits, was enjoying the activities. He and his brother were merrily making waves in the water in an attempt to sink their sister's boat. The two of them had always ganged up on her, but were no match for her temper. She, in turn, was endeavoring to ram their boats with a reed she had plucked from the fountain's edge. Orla laughed along with her children and avoided the splashing by standing off to the side under her parasol.

Presently, a page boy appeared with a note for the King. Olav wiped his hands dry and gave the note a brief glance before looking up at Orla and handing it to her. She raised a brow but took the note and read it. She could not help the smile that graced her lips upon reading the missive.

Orla excused herself from her husband and children and made her way into the palace, intent on completing some errands before granting her returning Captain an audience. She stopped in at the kitchens to personally order a tray with food and drinks delivered to her sitting room. Then she visited the great hall and asked their butler to please escort the Captain to the sitting room once he had been settled back in his rooms. Having completed her tasks, she went to her own bedroom and studied her reflection in the mirror before removing her outdoor hat and taming some of the tendrils of hair that had escaped her braid. She was still quite beautiful, her hair not dulled but merely speckled with gray. Her cheeks and nose were dotted with freckles and her face showed a wisdom gleaned from years as the Queen. Satisfied in her appearance, she entered her sitting room and sat on the edge of a chair as she waited.

Shortly, there was a knock on the door and she rose to answer it herself, having dismissed her maids in favor of privacy.

"Your Majesty, Captain Ciarán Allyn," the butler announced as he bowed.

"Thank you." She nodded to the butler and he excused himself. "Captain Allyn, do come in and be comfortable," she said politely.

Ciarán bowed. "Your Majesty, it is a pleasure to see you." He smiled at her, kissed the top of her hand, and sat on the settee next to the fire.

"I trust your journey was not too harrowing. Do you have any news?" she asked.

Ciarán coughed for a moment. Orla frowned but waited patiently for him to begin. He cleared his throat. "Indeed, your brother the King, sends his warmest regards. He has sent you and your children gifts. With your permission, I will distribute them to the appropriate servants in your household so that you may receive them at your leisure. I had—" His speech was interrupted by yet another cough.

"Captain, are you ill?" Orla asked, attempting to keep the alarm out of her voice.

Ciarán smiled and shook his head. "Nay, it is but a minor thing that should resolve shortly. Might I have a drink to soothe my throat?"

"Of course, stay and let me fetch it." Orla jumped up and poured him a glass of the Kingdom of Eiremor's finest whiskey. If asked, she would say she preferred the drink, but in reality, she kept it on hand for Ciarán because she knew he preferred it over the spirits found in this kingdom. She handed him the glass and he took a hearty swig then gave her an appreciative smile.

"There, right as rain," he said reassuringly.

"Ciarán," she warned.

"I'm perfectly fine. I am just tired from the journey. Riding so many days straight is not as easy as it once was. I am getting to be an old man," he joked.

"Please, do not remind your Queen of her age, it is impolite," she retorted.

Ciarán chuckled.

"Perhaps you could tell me how the family has been faring these long weeks I was away, while I rest a moment."

He looked at her with exaggerated expectation and it was all she could do not to laugh. She watched him closely for a moment and then relented to both her laughing and his request.

Orla began by telling him all about the kittens that were born in the stables, and how they piled onto Quinn the moment they saw him, and then proceeded to run after him if he tried to escape the barn. He swore that they were after him, but after a day or so, he became sullen if they did not follow him around the yard. Quinn had scrounged up a length of twine and would swing it about for them to attack, often from his shoulders and once from his head. Orla healed the scratch the kitten left in his ear and he had run right back to the stables to play a new game with the kittens.

She relayed how Runa was beginning to show an interest in traveling to other kingdoms on what she termed "diplomatic" missions, but Orla secretly realized they were just a disguise for Runa's romantic notions of adventures waiting to happen. The child was restless and it did not help that Erik reminded her that she should begin acting like *a proper lady* now, since she was getting older. Runa retaliated by interrupting one of his sword fighting lessons and beating him soundly while the tutor was too afraid to tell her she could not fight in a dress.

She recounted the events of Erik's first council meeting— he had come of age—and the preparations that Olav was taking to discuss marriage possibilities with their son. Erik was resisting the idea of having to rule once Olav was gone. He did not want to believe his father would leave him such responsibilities. Being the heir, Erik had responsibilities and he was well-educated for them. Orla remembered a time when she, herself, was not ready to face the facts of what being royal meant to her kingdom, so she forgave him his hesitance.

"Today, Olav was teaching them to sail boats in the fountains. Do you remember that time we raced boats with Lochlann and Kellan?" she asked.

Ciarán chuckled. "The time you cheated?"

Orla gasped at the implication. "I most certainly did not!"

"Aye, you did. You used magic to make the wind blow yours farther. Lochlann's boat was winning, fair and square."

"I was just using my strengths to my advantage." Orla smiled at the memory. "You threw mud on me."

"I was defending my brother and it would have continued but Kellan ran off and told our mothers what was happening." Ciarán remembered his mother's fury on finding out he had assaulted the Princess. "My mother made sure I never forgot my place again."

Orla frowned. "Is that why you weren't allowed to play with me without a guard after that?"

"Aye, Mother said we were getting too old to be with the princess alone. People would talk and it would reflect poorly on her." Ciarán sighed.

"Hmm. Looks like we both learned lessons that day. My mother made sure I never used magic merely for the purposes of getting my own way again. She made me help in the kitchens for a week and no magic was allowed. I still hate peeling potatoes!" Orla looked at him with mirth in her eyes.

"So *that* is why the mash was all lumpy that week!" Ciarán laughed and ducked the pillow thrown at his head.

Orla and Ciarán changed the subject to other matters. They both made little plates from the refreshments that had been brought to the sitting room and ate while they discussed her brother and the refurbishments he was making to the castle in Eiremor. Ciarán told her of the grand designs Kellan had for the unused meadow and she silently lamented the fact that it might no longer be the untamed wilderness of her youth.

ETERNAL WILLOW

After they finished eating, Orla entertained him with the story of one of the barons who had bought a magic potion to restore his wife to her youthful beauty. Little did the man know, the potion actually just made the wife think those around her were young and virile and the woman had run off with the man's seventy-year-old father.

Throughout the tale, Ciarán's eyes had grown heavier and heavier until he had finally fallen asleep to the sound of her voice. Orla frowned as she watched him doze. Time had been relatively kind to them both and he was still as handsome as he had been in his youth. His once jet black hair was now gray at the temples and speckled gray throughout the rest; it had the effect of making him look distinguished and wise. His scruff, too, was dabbled with gray, yet he still maintained it in a length to suggest some nonchalance on his part, though she knew it required diligent daily maintenance. The scar running down the right side of his face, from his eyebrow to his cheekbone, was less harsh than it had once been, but still a reminder of what he had endured in his life. She knew there were other scars—many of them much deeper—that she could not see and she shuddered at the memory.

What she did not like to see were the dark circles clearly evident underneath his eyes. Nor did she like the slight wheezing sound that she could hear as he breathed. Orla was sure he was not well and doing his best to hide it. The man was rather stubborn and tried to protect her from harsh truths, even when she knew he was lying. He devoted his entire life to protecting her, but he never understood she was stronger than she looked and wanted to be the one to protect *him*. She felt she owed him that much for all his years of selfless service.

After watching him for some time, Orla roused Ciarán.

"My apologies, majesty. I should have paid you more focus. Please continue," Ciarán said with chagrin.

"Nonsense. You are clearly exhausted from your journey. Shall we see you at supper?" she asked politely.

Ciarán nodded. "Aye. Thank you for your hospitality."

"We are quite happy at your return, Ciarán. I do hope you will be able to rest and recover in due course." Orla smiled at him and dismissed him as he bowed and left the room.

Orla rang a bell and a maid entered the room.

"Your Majesty?" the maid asked.

"Please have my physician check in on Captain Allyn as soon as possible," Orla ordered her maid, who curtsied and left to do her mistress's bidding.

Ciarán sighed as he let the physician into his room.

"I'm surprised it took this long," he said.

The physician chuckled. "You know Her Majesty worries. How about we do a quick exam and I will let you get back to your unpacking."

Ciarán nodded. He removed his shirt while the physician set up his instruments. The physician listened to his heart and his breathing, checked his ears and nose and throat and then took Ciarán's pulse. After a moment, he hummed to himself.

"Well?" Ciarán asked with impatience.

"I believe it is just an allergy, but the wheezing does concern me. When did this begin?" the physician asked.

"About a month ago," Ciarán said.

The physician nodded. "Well, it could be more serious than allergies. I would suggest you rest in order to recuperate fully," the physician ordered.

"Aye, I will do my best. Please let Her Majesty know there is no cause for alarm." Ciarán patted the physician on the back.

The physician bowed and made his way out of the room. Ciarán stood for a long moment staring at the door before quietly walking over and cracking it a sliver. He smiled to himself as he heard Orla and the physician discussing his illness in quiet tones.

Ciarán shut the door and walked over to his window. Rain clouds had moved in and he was sure they were in for a raucous thunderstorm. He rubbed his left bicep absentmindedly in an attempt to soothe the cramps that always came with bad weather. Once the raindrops started pattering on the window, he turned to survey his open trunk. The arrival of the physician had pre-empted his unpacking and he wanted to finish before the supper bells rang.

When he came to the bottom of the trunk, Ciarán retrieved a small piece of parchment paper. He unwrapped the paper and gently laid the piece of tree branch and leaves aside. He rubbed his fingers over the etching he had done of the carving from the tree. Having inspected both the branch and the parchment, he replaced the branch and folded it inside the parchment. Then he tied a ribbon around the four edges and laid the whole package inside a wooden box on his writing desk.

He began coughing again and so he resolved to lay down and rest until supper. The rain pounded the windows and the thunder shook the castle as he slept and dreamed.

chapter two

then

Ciarán ran from the castle followed closely by Lochlann, whom he had been trying to escape in the first place. He wanted to vomit; this was surely a cruel joke and all would be right in a moment. He would wake up and find that it was nonsense and there was no cause for alarm. He ran as fast as he could until he reached the willow tree and the lake, tossing the long branches aside and throwing himself against the trunk. He hid his face in his arms, embarrassed that he could not keep it together. It would not do him any good to let Lochlann see him crying and he fought back the tears threatening to erupt at any moment. Soon, he felt a hand on his back and he held his breath.

"Please talk to me. She was my mother too," Lochlann said in a soft voice.

Ciarán's muffled voice responded, "She can't be gone. What will I do? You are leaving and I will be alone."

Lochlann sighed and sat down. He stared at the water

with unseeing eyes. He did not know what to say to his brother. After choking back his emotions, Ciarán also sat down, trying to avoid facing his brother with his red eyes and blotchy cheeks. He turned his face as far away as possible in his seated position.

Lochlann took a deep breath. "They have promised you will have a place here. They promised her. I would not leave if you did not have a home. I will not be gone long and when I return I will find us a place together."

"You can't give up everything for me," Ciarán said.

"I know but I want to help you," Lochlann told him. "You are my only family and I will make sure we always have each other. You are never alone."

"Lochlann, I feel so lost. I thought she would get better." Ciarán finally lost the battle with his tears and they streamed down his face.

Ciarán locked his arms around his legs and hid his face in his knees. Lochlann hugged Ciarán as he sobbed and rubbed soothing circles on his back. His own tears ran unchecked down his cheeks. Ciarán had always struggled with wanting to be just like him but always being just a little too far behind in age. Their mother had been the only person who could calm his wild urges.

She had a fondness for her youngest son that had sometimes left Lochlann feeling jealous. Once, in a fit of temper, he asked his mother why she cared more for Ciarán than himself. She'd sat him down and replied that Lochlann did not need her attention as much as Ciarán did because Lochlann was sure of his place in the world, whereas his brother was still adrift. Lochlann understood and, from that moment on he'd tried to help steer his brother in the right direction. Lochlann worried that the loss of their mother would leave his brother in a perilous state. He knew that was why his mother asked the queen to look after them.

After what felt like an eternity, the sobs subsided and Ciarán straightened up with embarrassment. He avoided his brother's gaze until Lochlann put a hand under his chin and waited for their eyes to meet.

"I promise I will always make sure you have a home and I will always be your brother, so don't think you are ever alone. I've got your back. King Phelan and Queen Meara promised me you would be well-cared for because they loved mother, too. We won't be parted for long and, when the time is right, you can join me in service." Lochlann waited until Ciarán nodded.

Lochlann looked over Ciarán's shoulder and smiled. "Best dry your eyes. I will delay her as much as I possibly can," Lochlann said as he stood.

Ciarán straightened up and quickly swiped at his eyes. He scrubbed his face and discreetly sniffled. He heard someone coming in the grass behind him.

"I'm so sorry for your loss, Lochlann," Orla said as she hugged him.

"Thank you, Your Highness," he said.

"Let's not worry about titles today. Today you are my brother. I am here for you if you need to talk, as is Kellan. Is it okay for me to talk to him?" she asked and they both glanced at Ciarán.

Lochlann nodded. "Aye, I think it would help." He hugged her again and began walking back to the castle.

Orla took a deep breath and moved the branches of the tree aside. She observed Ciarán's still form, his head leaning against the tree with his eyes closed, seemingly nonchalant. She waited a moment and then sat next to him, mimicking his posture. She attempted to keep her breathing even while she waited for him to speak first. Her heart ached for Ciarán, she could not imagine losing her mother or father and he had now lost both. He took a deep breath and then let it out in a huff.

"Your parents are very kind. Lochlann has told me they have offered to let me stay," he said.

Orla opened her eyes and looked at him with confusion.

"Of course they did. Your mother was a great friend and

confidante to mine," she said.

"Aye, she had no enemies," he said as he fought another bout of tears.

Orla grabbed his hand and he linked their fingers together. She squeezed them in reassurance.

"You will always have a home with us, Ciarán." She was fighting tears of her own.

Ciarán nodded and Orla leaned her head on his shoulder. She rubbed her thumb lightly across his, trying to convey all she could not say.

"Do you mind if we just sit and not talk?" he asked.

Orla shook her head. She closed her eyes again and allowed her tears to fall silently down her cheeks. She could feel him shaking and squeezed his hand. It was the only way she knew how to show him some measure of comfort, for in the end there were no words that would soothe the ache of losing his mother at such a young age. His mother had been *his* most trusted confidant, too.

For the rest of the afternoon, they sat under the willow tree, watching the wind gently blowing the flowers in the meadow and listening to the birds singing above them. They stayed until well after sunset, when the night grew chilly and Orla began to shiver. Ciarán helped her up and they walked hand-in-hand back to the castle.

Ciarán became a much quieter person after his mother's death. Lochlann stayed at the castle until the prescribed mourning period passed. The weight of the responsibility for his younger brother was now on his shoulders and he, too, changed. He made the final leap from child to adult. He fussed over Ciarán those first weeks and it had led to several outbursts from his younger brother.

Ciarán could not blame his sibling; they both were

dealing with the grief in their own ways. However, Ciarán had felt a small measure of relief when it came time for him to leave for his commission on the Royal Armada's newest ship. Ciarán refused to go to the docks to see Lochlann off, preferring to say their farewells at the castle. Lochlann promised to write often and Ciarán merely nodded his head, unable to say anything for fear he might embarrass himself by begging his brother to stay.

Ciarán was assigned new rooms in the castle, in the same wing as Orla and Kellan. He knew it was only practical; his family of three had become one in a very short time and Lochlann would not need rooms for most of the year. When he did visit, while on leave, he could either share with Ciarán or be given a guest room. Practicality aside, he missed the special loving touch his mother had given their old rooms.

Despite Lochlann's declarations to the contrary, Ciarán felt so alone. It was as if he were constantly being punched in the gut. It just would not let him sleep.

Queen Meara tried to console her dearly departed friend's children as best she could, given her other royal duties. It was a balm to Lochlann, but she knew it was not enough for Ciarán. He had been so used to having his mother to discuss his day, and to work out his issues— losing her was a deep blow. Ciarán was not in the habit of showing his emotions so easily in front of others, especially not to his sovereign.

Several weeks after Lochlann left, Ciarán was mindlessly staring out the windows overlooking the harbor when a light knock came from the sitting room door. Ciarán sighed and went to open it, expecting Orla's visit to try to cheer him up, as was her usual routine of late. He believed she had taken him on as a charity case and the visits were becoming clockwork in their timing.

To his surprise, Queen Meara stood on the other side and he bowed deeply. He ran a hand through his hair and checked his clothing. He had not bothered dressing up as he did not intend to leave his rooms.

"Your Majesty, my apologies, I did not expect you. I am not presentable," he said.

Meara smiled, reached out to help him straighten and said, "Ciarán, may we talk?"

Ciarán nodded and watched as Meara directed a page boy to bring in a small chest. The boy set the chest on a table then bowed, taking his leave. Ciarán swallowed heavily, staring at it, then remembered his visitor and his manners.

"Would you like to sit?" he asked.

"Thank you," Meara said as she sat on the settee, smoothing her skirts around her. She studied Ciarán with sly sideways glances. The boy was losing weight and was very pale. She would talk to Phelan to see if he could get Ciarán interested in something besides moping.

Ciarán stood there waiting for her to speak. She looked at him and patted the spot next to her. He thought for a moment, then sat, feeling a bit awkward next to the Queen. His mother had been very devoted to Meara and spoke kindly of her, but Ciarán never felt comfortable alone in her royal presence. He was sure she probably would not notice him if not for his mother.

"Ciarán, we have not spoken much since your mother's death. I would hope to remedy that today. She was my dearest friend and I would hate to think you might be suffering without anyone to comfort you. How are you doing? Orla tells me you have not been out of your rooms much."

"I..." Ciarán sighed. "I am well, Your Majesty. I prefer my rooms to the sympathy from members of the court. Each conversation reminds me of her. I don't want to hear how much she was loved. I don't think I can handle it anymore."

Meara smiled. "Please, Ciarán, I wish to be your friend. Losing a parent is very hard at any age, but especially when we are young. I cannot imagine what you have experienced in losing both of your parents. Did you know I lost my father when I was very young?"

Ciarán shook his head.

"I was about five when my father was killed in a training incident. It was very difficult for me. I worshipped him and suddenly he was no longer there for me to talk to whenever I wished. My mother and I were never close. I was close to my father's mother but after his death, I felt like she only ever saw him when she looked at me. Suddenly, she and I no longer spent as much time together as we had before he died. It was too painful for her. I felt very lonely for a long time."

Meara watched as Ciarán seemed to struggle with a question.

"Lochlann was closer to father. I suppose it was because he was older and just like father. But mother... she was... she understood me. It was as if she knew what I thought before I even had the chance to think it. She didn't let me doubt myself and now that is all I do." Ciarán felt his eyes tearing up for what seemed the thousandth time.

Meara put her arm around him. She laid his head on her shoulder and held him there.

"Your mother loved both of you very much. I loved her as if she were my own sister and I was privileged to know her. She would not want you to lose yourself merely because she is gone. Your mother would want you to remember her and honor her memory by continuing to be a gracious and gentle young man. Locking yourself away will not honor her memory."

Ciarán sniffled, "I just don't know what to do. I am alone now and—"

Meara interrupted. "Ciarán Allyn, as long as you live in my kingdom, you will never be alone. Do you know what I promised your mother?"

Ciarán shook his head.

"Your mother never asked for anything from me until the day she died. She called for me and I went because she was my closest friend. On that day, I was not her Queen. She said, 'Please take care of my boys like they were your own sons. Especially, Ciarán, he will need your support with Lochlann gone. Please love them as I have.'"

Ciarán's tears ran down his cheeks and he looked away. Meara gently turned his face back towards hers. She looked him in the eyes.

"Ciarán, I have always loved you and your brother. It was not a hard promise to make. You are as dear to me as my own children. Do you understand?"

He nodded and she hugged him, waiting patiently for his tears to subside. He finally straightened and gave her a look full of sheepish gratitude.

"Now, I have some things to show you" she said.

She rose and went to retrieve the chest from the table. He watched her with interest. He should have asked her if she needed help, but his curiosity had gotten the better of him, and he momentarily forgot his manners.

"Your mother left this in my safekeeping and I think it is time I return it to you. Let's have a look."

Meara opened the chest and began pulling out things Ciarán recognized as belonging to his mother. At last, she came to a small green pouch. She opened it and a silver necklace with a pendant fell into her hand. Ciarán's eyes widened when he saw the necklace.

"But that is mother's pendant. The last one father gave to her before he was killed. I thought she was wearing it on the pyre," he said in awe.

Meara nodded. "Yes. She asked me to make sure it was removed before the pyre was lit. She wanted you to have it. She said when the time was right you would know what to do with it."

Ciarán picked up the necklace, inspecting the pendant he knew so well. Made of green ammolite in a silver setting, the stone changed colors as he moved it in the light, just like his mother's eyes. She told him it was one of the reasons his father had given it to her: it captured the fire of her eyes.

Ciarán closed his eyes at the memory and, for the first time in months, a smile appeared on his face. He was glad to have such a small but meaningful piece of her.

"I will let you look through the rest on your own. Please come to me or Phelan if you need anything. We are your family if you will have us," Meara said as she rose.

"Thank you. For everything you have done and for giving me this part of her," Ciarán said.

"You are most welcome, sweetheart," she said as she patted his shoulder and moved towards the door.

Just as she was leaving, she added as an afterthought, "I will talk to Phelan and we will see if we can get you out of these rooms. Orla is likely waiting to see you. She thinks I do not know about her daily visits. I think she misses her old friend."

At that, she was gone. Ciarán looked down at the necklace and smiled. He clasped it tightly in his hand, offering up a small thanks to his mother, wherever she may be. He then jumped up with renewed purpose and set off to find Orla.

chapter three

Ciarán had been home for little more than a week when he finally took tea with Orla in the castle gardens. The gardens were one of her favorite places and she could be found there most days when the weather cooperated. Olav had taken special care to bring some of the plants, flowers, and trees from Eiremor to Fadersogn especially for her. He had even constructed a small pond with a much smaller version of the willow tree that she seemed to love so much. It was not an exact replica of the lands of her youth, but close enough that she felt the most peace in this personal sanctuary.

She was disturbed to learn Ciarán's cough was still present, despite his obvious efforts at containing it, going so far as to clear his throat more often and chew on an herb the physician prescribed to alleviate the urge. The herb was very bitter and made just about all of his food and drinks almost unbearably bland, but if it kept the physicians out of his rooms, it was worth every bite. Orla knew better than to mention it yet again; she pushed her luck in sending the physician in the first place, even though he reassured her Ciarán merely suffered from an allergy or an early autumn cold that would resolve itself shortly. At the current moment, her concerns over the cough were superseded by a discussion, which some would call an argument, about the necessity of yet another diplomatic mission on behalf of the King.

"But you've only been home a week," Orla said angrily, throwing her napkin down in a huff.

"Aye, however, His Majesty said this cannot wait," Ciarán replied gently.

Orla stood. "Does it always have to be you?"

Ciarán sighed and stood as well, deferring to both her gender and his station. "Your Majesty..."

"Don't!" she shook her head.

"Orla? This is my job. I have no family and, therefore, I am dispensable. It is my duty to the kingdom and what I agreed to when I took the position in your court. I am a trusted advisor and Olav needs me for this mission." He tried to make her see his side of the matter, but sighed when he saw her lower lip trembling.

"You... you are not dispensable. The children love you as if you were their own blood." Orla was trying to bite back her own emotions with great difficulty.

Ciarán smiled. "Aye and their 'Uncle C' plans to keep them safe. However, there is hardly any danger in this trip. I am merely taking urgent correspondence to Noregfjord. It is not even that far. I shall return in four days at most."

"You are unwell and the weather in Noregfjord will be turning to hard winter any day now."

"I am fine Orla. The physician has cleared me for travel. I see nothing to prevent me from carrying out my duties. You shall see I am right upon my speedy return." Ciarán gave her a cocky grin and she could not contain the smile that it induced.

"I am just not sure that it should be you who goes. We

have plenty of capable messengers. I have need of you here and you are *my* Captain," she replied stubbornly.

"Your Majesty, with respect, I volunteered for the mission. I promise I will return," he said.

Orla gasped at his words and looked away. She muttered under her breath.

"I've heard *that* before."

Ciarán winced and tried to pretend he had not heard her. He schooled his face into a mask of calm before she looked back at him.

"Four days, Your Majesty, that is all, and I will come back," he said with sympathy.

Orla gave a long-suffering sigh, as if it were a great burden for her to relent. "Very well. Four days, Captain."

Ciarán bowed. "As you wish."

Orla watched him go, then sat heavily in her chair. She felt like something was not right, as if there were a tiger lurking in the bushes ready to pounce. She shook herself to clear her mind, fearing those thoughts alone would somehow produce the beast in question. With unsteady hands, she poured another cup of tea.

Runa heard of the imminent departure to Noregfjord and was waiting in the hallway outside of Ciarán's rooms when he returned to them. She straightened from the wall quickly and put on her most winning smile. She smoothed out her skirts, standing taller. She was hoping to charm him into letting her go on the trip.

Ciarán noticed her and sighed. Runa was a beautiful girl full of spunk and wit. She would make a very interesting wife one day, and would need a husband who saw her as an equal or she would stomp all over him. However, as much as he admired those qualities, which reminded him of her mother, he didn't necessarily want them aimed at him when he was the one standing in the way of what she wanted.

"Uncle Ciarán, it is such a lovely day, is it not?" she asked in a pleasant voice.

"No," he said.

"What? Did the weather turn?" she asked innocently.

"Runa, as much as I would love to stand here all day and exchange pleasantries, I must pack for my trip. Let's dispense with the buttering and tell me what you want. I am sure the answer will still be no."

Runa pouted. "Fine. Can you please take me with you?"

Ciarán shook his head and was about to speak when Runa threw her arms around him and looked up at him with puppy dog eyes.

"*Please* take me with you. I am so desperate to leave the castle and see something of the world. We are friends with Noregfjord are we not? It isn't winter yet, so the passage is not treacherous. Please take me. I am sure father and mother would be okay if I was with you. I can ride in pants and I won't slow you down," she gushed, hardly taking a breath in between sentences.

Ciarán pried her arms from around his middle.

"Runa, I promised your mother this would be a quick trip. She is not pleased I am going. If I took you along, it would add time I am not at liberty to waste. You are not accustomed to riding as hard as I will have to in order to complete this in four days."

Runa crossed her arms and huffed.

"This is not fair."

"Aye Princess, I agree. However, I am a man of my word. Perhaps we can work on your parents for the next trip." He bowed and began to enter his rooms.

"I hate you!" Runa yelled and stomped away.

He watched after her retreating figure, shaking his head. Ciarán smiled, thinking 'like mother, like daughter' and closed the door.

Olav and Ciarán were discussing final instructions when Orla entered. Both men looked up and she waved them off, indicating they should finish their conversation. Ciarán pocketed the missive to the King of Noregfjord and then made to leave the room.

"Might we have a moment, Captain Allyn?" Orla said as he was leaving.

Olav looked at his wife and saw the pleading in her eyes. He nodded and quietly left the room. Orla sat in a chair and waited for Ciarán to do the same. She took a moment to gather her thoughts.

"I don't like this," she began.

Ciarán sighed. "We have already been over this."

Orla nodded. "I know. But something's not right. I can feel it. You know I would not tell you this if I did not truly believe that this trip has some danger to it. I would prefer if you delayed the trip until a later date or have Olav send someone else."

"I can't do that. His Majesty is counting on me delivering this missive. He needs someone he can trust and I am that man. I can't delay on an uneasy feeling you might have about it. You always hate it when I leave for more than a trip to the village."

Orla stood abruptly and began pacing the room. Ciarán watched her and felt bad that he was the source of her agitation. However, he had a job to do and he could not always stop on her whims alone.

"Four days and I will be back," he said.

Orla stopped in her tracks as a shiver ran down her spine.

"You know I've heard those words before. Please don't say them now, not this time," she whispered.

Ciarán swallowed. "We are not at war, Orla, this is not

the same. It is a quick trip and after I will rest as requested, I promise. I am sure His Majesty can find something for me to do within Fadersogn's borders for a while."

"So you are determined then?" Orla turned and stared at him.

"Aye."

Orla nodded. "Very well, Captain. You may go."

Ciarán stood and almost reached out to her but thought better of it at the last minute. He picked up his maps and strode purposefully out of the room.

Orla sent up a silent prayer to whatever Gods might be listening he return as promised.

chapter four

then

L ife had continued in the palace and Ciarán had slowly settled into his new reality. Orla and Kellan both received instruction in swordsmanship, history, diplomacy and other pursuits required of noble children. Ciarán was given the same access to these tutors along with them and he was proving to be an apt pupil. On days that Orla received special instruction in running a household, Kellan and Ciarán would pursue other endeavors such as hunting or archery. The bonds he shared with them grew stronger as the days passed.

Ciarán was alone only when the siblings had magic lessons.

Orla and Kellan both had magic; however, Orla's appeared to be stronger. Magic practitioners were rare in the known kingdoms. It manifested in one of two ways: through the children of true love—and given most marriages were arranged, this was the rarest type of magic—or through an unknown luck of birth. At one time, in the long ago history of the world, magic flourished, but as the centuries passed, magic appeared to die out and become scarce to the point that almost no one really remembered it, save those rare folk who still had it.

Each person with magic appeared to possess a unique form of it. For instance, Kellan's magic gave him the ability to manipulate nature. Orla was unique in that she had been gifted with several forms of magic. She had shown the ability to influence nature, see into the future, and manipulate elements. Small groups of practicing magicians formed schools and communes in order to pass on their wisdom and learn from each other. Queen Meara had sent for a tutor from a nearby school when her children were discovered to have magic. They now had a full-time, in-house magical consultant who was in charge of teaching the siblings how to use their magic wisely and justly.

In addition to his studies, Ciarán spent more time in the company of King Phelan. He did not have any real reasons for being in council meetings and royal audiences, save the King's own indulgence of his curiosity. He was like a sponge and, on occasion, provided very good insight to the King on one issue or another. He enjoyed receiving news first hand of the Royal Armada and specifically, his brother's ship. Phelan took a special interest in him and attempted to groom him for service as a Royal Councilor. Kellan would need good advisors when Phelan was gone.

Ciarán had also begun to notice how Orla was growing into an even more beautiful young woman. She had lost the chubbiness from her childhood, and her eyelashes were long and black, providing a stark contrast to her pale cheeks. Her love of the outdoors had given her a speckling of light brown freckles across both her cheeks and her nose. She was breathtaking when she smiled.

If he were being truthful, he would admit he had always been attracted to her, even when they had their differences. Orla was a spitfire and very much carried her own opinions. She was quick to defend her point of view when she believed she was wronged and passionate about almost everything else. She was strong and she intrigued him.

One spring day, Ciarán found her lying in a meadow in one of her best dresses. He smirked and stood over her.

"Does your mother know you are out here?" he asked playfully.

Orla stuck her tongue out at him. Ciarán chuckled and sat down next to her. He began plucking the purple flowers around him and weaving them into a crown. As his hands worked, he hummed a sea shanty Lochlann had taught him. It was one he was told his mother had been fond of since his father used to sing it to her.

"Ciarán?' Orla asked as she sat up.

He looked at her with a raised brow, waiting for her to continue.

Orla sighed and looked away. "Do you ever wish we had a different life?"

"What do you mean?" he asked.

"What if I were not a princess? I mean, what if I grew up in the village and was the daughter of a pirate instead of a King? Do you think my life would be better?" she asked.

Ciarán thought a moment, trying to figure out what she actually meant. He thought she was content with her lot in life. He could not imagine being sad if he were a prince with both of his parents still living. It seemed to him he would have many more options than joining the armada and living a life at sea. He might be able to pursue other careers if he had a choice and money were no issue.

Orla waved her hand in front of his face. "Hello? Ciarán?"

He shook himself out of his thoughts.

"I don't think I follow. Why would you not want to be who you are? You have your parents, your brother, everything you could want. Are you unsatisfied with living here?"

Orla shook her head. "Yes... I mean no. Well, not quite."

Ciarán laughed and she swatted at him.

"What I am trying to say is, I just don't know if I am ready to start having suitors and thinking about being a queen. Mother has been hounding me about my birthday ball next year. She has been giving me extra lessons on filling a dance card and learning all the names of the Princes from neighboring kingdoms. All the extra etiquette is killing me. It is so tedious," she said.

"I see."

"Do you?"

"Yes, but I don't think you have to worry so much. You will find a suitor who can keep up with you."

Ciarán frowned slightly at that thought. In truth, it made him jealous to think of the person who might capture her heart. He did not want to admit it, but he had dreams of winning her and marrying her himself. Dreams he should not be having as he was well below her in station.

Orla sighed and flopped backward dramatically.

"You are no help."

"Ok, how about this: you will rebel and become a pirate princess and sail the high seas. Men will shake in their boots at your name and you will die an old maid having never found a man worthy of your spirit," he said cheekily.

Orla sat back up and studied him a moment. Then she gave him a sly smile and snatched the flower crown from his hands.

"Queen Orla of the High Seas, I like the sound of that. But who says no man will be worthy of me? Perhaps I already know who he is? I have been working on prophecy magic lately," she replied.

"Oh? Well then, Your Majesty." He gave a mock bow as best he could while seated. "I am your most humble servant for all time."

Orla got an odd expression on her face and a shiver raced through her.

Orla remembered her lessons the previous week. She and her tutor had been exploring prophecy magic. Orla thought it was exciting she might be able to see the future. Kellan would be so jealous and she could counteract her mother's machinations on the subject of her marriage because she would already know who she would marry.

Orla had asked her tutor to teach her how to hone her requests so that she could see the visions more clearly. He had warned her that prophecy magic was not something to play with. Often times, the practitioner might not like what she sees.

"Is it set in stone then?" she asked.

The tutor shook his head. "No, my Princess, but the outcomes are nearly often the same. It is very hard to change our fate once it has been set into motion."

"I want to see!" she demanded.

"Very well. Think of your question clearly in your mind and search for the answer. Your gift should allow you to be an observer of the future you ask about."

Orla thought her question. "Does Ciarán ever kneel before me?" It was a silly question for, of course, she knew one day he would propose.

Instantly she saw herself as if floating above her body, she was older but not too much older. She was sitting on a throne next to another man, who was not her father. A worn, broken looking Ciarán was kneeling in front of her, head bowed.

He looked up and said, "I offer my service to your Majesties, your most humble and loyal servant."

Orla gasped and was jolted back to her study room. She ran out of the room, ignoring the calls from her tutor.

"Are you cold?" Ciarán asked with concern.

She shook her head. "No. Just a weird sense of something, but it has passed. Let's talk of something else." Orla internally chided herself. It was just an unclear vision. Her tutor told her that visions were not always set in stone.

Ciarán gave her a look but let the subject drop. The rest of the afternoon they gave into the fantasy that she was a pirate queen and he was a noble she'd kidnapped. At the end of the day, Ciarán felt happy but had the foreboding sense that his childhood was coming to an end.

Lochlann was finally coming home for a visit and Ciarán eagerly watched the harbor from his window. There was a slight chill in the air and he was wrapped in a blanket from his bed to ward it off, only his face peeking out of it. Ciarán wanted for nothing at the palace but he was reluctant to ask for anything, so his current winter wardrobe was lacking. He made a mental note to procure for himself an extra blanket to plug the drafts from the window during the coming winter months. He also needed a better coat.

Presently, he saw the white sails of Lochlann's ship moving into the harbor. The *Emerald Sea* was truly one of the jewels of the Armada. It was fast and sleek, designed by the King himself. Lochlann was incredibly honored to serve on that particular ship and he suspected that his mother's friendship with the Queen had something to do with it.

It would be another hour or so before the ship docked and Ciarán used some of that time to bathe and put on his best attire. He dressed himself carefully in a blue shirt, black waistcoat and black breeches. He had polished his shoes and had his hair cut. He wanted Lochlann to see that he kept himself well and presentable in the time they were apart. He did not want his brother to spend more time than necessary worrying about him.

Ciarán made his way down to the village to await his brother's departure from the ship. Orla and Kellan offered to accompany him but he wanted to see his brother alone for this first reunion. He was unsure if he could keep his emotions in check and did not want an audience. His greatest fear was disappointing his brother in some way and did not want his closest friends to be a witness to his shame, if that were the case.

The docks were busy. Final preparations were being made for the winter months and merchant ships were off-loading provisions that would sustain the kingdom during the embargo created by the frozen waters. Icebergs were a real danger, and the King and Queen long ago decided it was better to stock supplies for the winter, rather than risk importing anything and losing a ship.

Early during their reign, a particularly bad winter resulted in the loss of not one, but two ships from their kingdom and the lives of several hundred men. They, personally, compensated the families of each crew member despite the fact that they were not responsible for the deaths. It won them the everlasting gratitude of both the families and their subjects.

Ciarán stepped quickly out of the way of a horse and flatbed carriage loaded with crates, but he was not quick enough to dodge the splash of muddy water the carriage splashed in his direction. He grumbled when he looked down to see his previously pristine stockings were now splattered in a way that would not be easy to clean off before Lochlann arrived. Nevertheless, he attempted to wipe off the worst of it.

He looked up quickly when he heard a hearty chuckle to find that Lochlann had disembarked and found him. Ciarán frowned and then took a moment to study his brother. Lochlann seemed to have grown taller and become darker and more muscular from his days spent on deck. He looked much more like a man than the eighteen-year-old teenager who'd left all those months ago.

"Always getting yourself in a mess, huh, little brother?" Lochlann said jovially.

"I was fine until a moment ago and I am not little." Ciarán frowned.

Lochlann put his hand on Ciarán's shoulder and waited for the latter to straighten up. He looked into his brother's eyes for a moment, then a wide grin spread on his face. He pulled Ciarán into a bone-crushing hug and pat his back.

"So good to see you!" he exclaimed.

Ciarán nodded, laughing despite himself. "You were missed, brother. How is life at sea?"

"Not bad. I do miss real food though. After the first few days, fresh vegetables and meat run out and we are forced onto sea rations." At that, a mock shudder ran through Lochlann. "So tell me, how is life in the castle?"

"It is different, but I have adjusted. I am diligent in my studies and I hope I have also learned something by attending the King when he requires my service. I only wish to make you proud, Lochlann," Ciarán said hopefully.

Lochlann smiled and gestured that they should begin the journey back to the castle. Ciarán fell into step beside him, chewing his lip nervously until his brother answered his unspoken question.

"Ciarán, I am glad to see you well and it makes me happy to hear you are settled into castle life. Mostly, I am glad to be home and able to see you. I'm not certain you should worry about making me proud. It might be impossible for me to be more proud of you than I already am. His Majesty has written to me and is very impressed with your thinking skills and ability to learn quickly," he said.

Ciarán nodded and looked away a moment. They walked a few more steps in silence when he heard his brother's stomach rumble. Lochlann laughed.

"I'm starving for real food. Think Cook would give me a snack before dinner?" he asked sheepishly.

Ciarán nodded.

"I'm certain of it, she always had a soft spot for you. Follow me," he said as they hurried off to the castle.

Later that evening, after Lochlann had his fill of both an afternoon snack and dinner, at which he had regaled their Royal hosts with his exploits on the ship, Ciarán and Lochlann returned to Ciarán's rooms. Lochlann was given the choice of where he wished to stay during the winter and he had asked Ciarán his preference. Having been separated from his brother for so long, he requested an extra bed be brought into his rooms so they could share a room like they had before their mother passed. Lochlann agreed; they were now roommates again.

Lochlann perused the rooms and made a joke about Ciarán being so fastidious in his cleaning that His Majesty could eat off the floors. This made Ciarán blush to the tips of his ears as his near-obsessive need for order had always been a sticking point between the two. Lochlann noticed and attempted to defuse the embarrassment by picking up the closest thing at hand, which happened to be the small chest of their mother's things. Ciarán watched as he opened it and silently went through the items, picking one or two up, then replacing them until he came to the bag holding their mother's necklace. He looked at Ciarán as if to ask permission and, when the latter nodded, he opened the bag and let the necklace fall into his hand.

"It's the necklace Father gave to Mother," Ciarán said.

"How?" Lochlann asked.

"Queen Meara. Mother asked her to give it to us. You can keep it if you want since you are the oldest. I am sure that she would have wanted you to have something of hers."

Lochlann stroked the pendant with his thumb then looked up.

"Do you not want it?" he asked.

"I do want it. Actually, could I ask you a question?"

Suddenly he could not meet Lochlann's eyes.

"You can always ask me anything." Lochlann waited, curious what had Ciarán so embarrassed again.

In a rush, Ciarán said, "Orla's sixteenth birthday is coming up and I was hoping to give it to her but of course Mother may have wanted you to have it and I would not want to..."

"I think that is a splendid idea," Lochlann said.

"You do?"

"Aye, Mother loved Orla and I think she would be happy we gave her most prized possession to one so worthy," he replied.

Ciarán eyed Lochlann suspiciously. "Worthy?"

"Ciarán it is clear to me that you are in love with her. I assume you will want to marry her one day?"

Ciarán's eyes widened and he sucked in a huge breath, sending him into a coughing spell after he inhaled spit into his windpipe. Lochlann came over and slapped him on the back a few times before he could finally breathe again.

"I can't marry her!" he exclaimed.

Lochlann shrugged. "Why not?"

"Because!" he said.

"Because is not a reason. Use your words, Ciarán you are usually so eloquent. You are a talented young man. You would make her a good husband, would you not?" Lochlann asked.

Ciarán nodded. "Aye, but I am not of royal blood. Our mother was merely a lady-in-waiting to the Queen. I could not presume to rise above my station. Already, Queen Meara is grooming Orla to receive princes from other kingdoms at her birthday ball. *Princes*, Lochlann. She would not approve of me as her suitor."

"I think she would if she knew you were interested. The Queen was not of royal blood either, yet King Phelan chose her. Don't discount yourself too much, brother. I have seen some of the princes of other kingdoms in my ship's travels. Believe me when I say they are no match for Orla."

Lochlann smiled at him.

Ciarán sighed. "Be that as it may, I do not think she thinks of me in that manner anyway. I shouldn't have brought it up."

Lochlann stared at his brother as if he had grown two heads and, when Ciarán became uncomfortable, he broke eye contact and went to unpack his things, letting the matter drop. For now.

Ciarán had been looking all over the palace for Orla. Her birthday ball was the next day and he was hoping to have a moment alone with her before all the guests began arriving. He wanted to give her the necklace in private. His gift was not particularly expensive and it was an older style than the current fashions. His mother had cherished it, but he worried Orla would think it too boring or beneath her station. He was sure the visitors from other kingdoms would be bringing much more lavish gifts than his. It embarrassed him to think that she might not appreciate being given such a lowly gift.

After an hour of searching, he passed by the King's offices and heard the man shouting at a guard. He tried his best to rush past the office, but King Phelan shouted out his name. Ciarán took a deep breath and pushed the door open. He was wary when the King was in a foul mood. It was not often, but anyone on the wrong side of the King's good will was surely in for a sound tongue lashing. Ciarán tried to rack his brain for anything that he might have done to deserve such lashing.

"Your Majesty?" Ciarán bowed as he entered the room.

"None of that." King Phelan waved his hand as he dismissed the guard. "Have you seen Orla? She seems to have vanished into thin air. The guards are useless and

Meara is beside herself. Orla was supposed to have her final dress fitting."

Ciarán shook his head. "I, too, was looking. If you so desire, I can continue my search and perhaps ask Lochlann to join in?"

Phelan nodded. "Yes, I think it wise. I did see her this morning and she was none too pleased about Meara's plans for the day. Between you and I, she is not fond of the idea of a ball. Last thing she said to me was the high seas sounded grand and that she might take a ride."

Ciarán's eyes widened as a sudden thought hit him. He made his hurried goodbye to King Phelan and rushed off with promises of bringing the Princess back to him. Phelan just shook his head and muttered "Youth" under his breath as he went to find Meara and hopefully calm her down.

"Lochlann! *Lochlann!*" Ciarán shouted as he ran into his rooms.

"I'm right here brother, no need to shout." Lochlann came around the corner. "What's happening?"

Ciarán frantically looked for his cloak and grabbed the dagger he wore in his boot when they were out hunting.

"Hurry, get your cloak, we need to get to the harbor before she does something stupid."

Lochlann grabbed his brother's shoulders. "Slow down, before *who* does something stupid?"

Ciarán shook his head. "There is no time, I'll explain on the way. Come on!"

Ciarán rushed out of the door with Lochlann following behind in bewilderment.

Orla sat in a corner of the tavern, hidden in her cloak's hood, watching the men coming and going. Now that she'd decided to run away, she was sure she could find the right crew. She was not worried about her safety. She had magic and could protect herself. However, she did not want to get in with a crew of thieves, she wanted to sail with noble merchant men from some kingdom far away. If they could get her away from her kingdom, she could figure out what to do in the next port. She was just screwing up her courage to talk to a captain who seemed to meet her criteria, when the door to the tavern slammed open and a wild-eyed Ciarán rushed in, followed closely by a much calmer Lochlann.

Orla sighed and rolled her eyes, Ciarán could be so dramatic. She watched as he went straight to the barkeep and asked if he had seen her. The barkeep laughed at the ridiculous idea the Princess would be in his tavern. She almost laughed at the look of indignation on Ciarán's face. He was so mad he was beginning to turn purple. Lochlann was doing his best to try to calm down his brother, to no avail. He sat Ciarán down on a nearby bench and Orla waved her hand to cast a spell that would make her even less noticeable. She could not understand why he was so distraught. She only felt minorly guilty as she eavesdropped on their conversation.

"We will find her, brother. This was a crazy idea anyway. Orla would never shirk from her duties, she loves her family," Lochlann said.

Orla winced. She didn't think about how this would look to her parents. She'd merely wanted to be free.

"Aye, you are right. I was just so sure. When we were younger, she'd mentioned a fantasy such as this, and I just thought perhaps she'd finally summoned the courage to do it," Ciarán replied. "Shall we return and face His Majesty?"

Lochlann nodded. "Aye, they probably found her already."

Orla rose and walked by the two brothers, still under her cloaking spell. She brushed past Ciarán and he straightened, looking around. A strange spark had startled him, as if shocked from stocking feet on bare castle floors.

"What is it?" Lochlann asked. "Did you remember something?"

Ciarán shook his head. "Nothing. I just thought... oh, never mind, let's get back and face the music."

The brothers rose and left the tavern. They made it outside only to find Orla standing next to their horses with her own. She acted as if she had been there for hours waiting on them.

"Orla!" Ciarán gasped.

Orla smiled and was about to graciously accept defeat when he continued.

"What in the blazes are you doing here on your own? You are a royal Princess and should have an escort. What did you think you were doing?" his tirade seemed endless.

Lochlann looked between the two. "Ciarán" he said warningly.

Ciarán continued, "Get on that horse now and I will take you back to your father."

Orla lost it. "Enough! As you seem so willing to remind me, I AM the Royal Princess and you are NOT royalty. I give the orders here. I am quite capable of taking care of myself."

Orla swiftly mounted her horse and sped off. Ciarán huffed so loudly Lochlann thought he would expel a lung. They mounted their horses and took off after Orla.

They caught up to her as she jumped off her horse and entered one of the towers leading to the battlements. Ciarán was hot on her heels, yelling at her to stop because he was not finished talking to her. She pretended not to hear him and continued on her way. Lochlann rolled his eyes and went to take care of the horses. He knew better than to intervene while those two were arguing. Their strong wills clashed all too often.

"Orla, stop!" Ciarán shouted.

Orla spun around. *"You do not get to order me to do anything!"*

Ciarán stopped short and turned bright red.

"Do you understand what could have happened? You could have been kidnapped? Or worse!" he pleaded in a low voice.

"I was fine until you showed up and drew attention to me. No one would have known who I was. After that, how could I have successfully found a ship after you waltzed in and announced that 'Her Royal Highness' is missing?" she spat at him.

"So you were just going to run away? Not tell anyone? Not very noble, Orla! People here love you and it would have devastated your parents." He was beyond angry at her selfishness.

Orla spun to walk away and Ciarán reached out, grabbing her arm. She turned and got in his face.

"You are not my mother and not my father. You are not my boss, Ciarán. I don't need you to protect me."

She was poking at his chest in a rage, getting angrier each moment he did not move or bow to her will. At one time, they were of equal height, but now he had grown taller and it irked her in this moment.

"Yes you do!" he insisted weakly.

"No I don't!" she said, pushing at his chest.

Neither noticed how close to the edge of the wall they'd moved. In that moment of anger, Orla's magic lashed out, the resulting push of it making Ciarán lose his balance. He fell over the side of the battlement into a cart in the courtyard below.

"Ciarán!" Orla screamed in terror.

Lochlann ran from the stables at the distress in her voice and looked up to see her staring down from the wall in horror. He followed her eyes and saw the cart where his brother lay unconscious.

Ciarán stared out the window, sullenly watching the guests arriving for the ball. The previous day had not gone as he thought it should have. Now he would not only be deprived of giving Orla his meager gift but also dancing with her on her birthday. He had been practicing and thought to impress her with his knowledge of the Waltz. Instead, he was confined to his rooms with a head injury and broken ribs. Luckily the cart had contained some hay, yet to be unloaded, and it kept him from a much worse fate. He wallowed in self-pity and sighed for the hundredth time in an hour.

Lochlann looked up from his book. "We could still go. You seem able to stand without dizziness. You would just need to be careful."

Ciarán glanced over his shoulder then back out the window. His shoulders sagged. "She wouldn't want me there anyway."

Lochlann rolled his eyes and threw the book down. He walked over to Ciarán's wardrobe and opened it up to look for his formal clothes.

"What are you doing?" Ciarán asked.

"We are going. If I have to hear you sigh one more time, I might drill a hole in my head," Lochlann said, only half-joking. He could not take his brother's misery.

"Lochlann..."

"Get up and get dressed. Now," Lochlann said, standing with his arms crossed until Ciarán nodded in defeat and began to dress.

Orla thought her head might explode if she had to meet one more person. Thankfully the introductions had dwindled and the dancing had started. She was presently dancing with Prince Olav of Fadersogn. He was a pleasant fellow and seemed very knowledgeable about her kingdom.

News had spread of Ciarán's "fall," and Olav had kindly asked how her friend fared. He was the first prince to show any interest in her as a person and not as a princess. Orla tried her best not to let her guilt over the ordeal show on her face but she was failing miserably. Olav was the nicest person she had met so far and it helped keep her mind off Ciarán. Olav graciously dismissed the idea that she was to blame and she relaxed a little.

Lochlann discreetly helped Ciarán into the ballroom and near a banister that he could lean on. He knew the physicians ordered rest but he also knew his brother was entirely miserable and not just from the fall into the cart. Despite her part in the accident, Orla had not yet spoken to Ciarán and, of course, the latter blamed himself for overstepping his station. Lochlann sighed inwardly at the two, so caught up in their own minds that neither could see the truth about their feelings for the other. He hoped one day soon they would work it out, yet he knew he could not force it, they needed to make the realizations themselves and he could only nudge his brother in the right direction.

Orla spotted Ciarán and Lochlann and could not help the smile that graced her face. Olav noticed and watched her as she tried to focus on the dance and not give away her interest in the brothers. The moment she'd spied them, her entire being changed. She practically glowed with happiness.

"Your friend?" Olav asked with curiosity.

"What? Oh, yes, it seems he might be better after all," Orla said with no small amount of relief in her voice.

She knew she should apologize to Ciarán, but she was often too stubborn for her own good. If she acknowledged he was right about her running off and she should not have caused the argument, it would be a blow to her pride, and she could not bear the thought of admitting she was wrong.

Olav looked over at the brothers. The younger must be the one who was hurt; the older and taller brother seemed to be hovering a bit protectively. They were both tall and lean, with matching blue eyes. The older had brown hair while the younger's was jet black. He could see the resemblance. The older one was saying something to his brother, but he shrugged and seemed very wary. Olav would make it a point to get to know both men during his weeklong stay at the castle. The older brother, he knew, was in the King's navy, and he would be very interested in discussing nautical affairs with the man.

"Might you introduce me, Your Highness?" Olav asked.

Orla startled. She was preoccupied with her thoughts and turned her eyes from Ciarán who looked pale. It could have been so much worse. She could have killed him. She blushed as she realized she was staring at Ciarán instead of giving her attention to Olav.

"Absolutely." She gave Olav a winning smile. He gave a slight nod and put her arm in his.

Lochlann straightened and nudged his brother, nodding in the direction of the approaching couple. Ciarán took a solid breath and, as much as it pained him, pulled up to his full height. When Orla and Olav came to a stop in front of him, he graciously bowed low.

"Your Highness," he said, fighting the pain in both his head and chest. It nearly made him pass out, but his ego was already bruised, and he would not make a scene by passing out at the Princess's feet.

Orla frowned and glanced at Lochlann, who just shrugged and gave a small warning nod to her. It would do no good for the two of them to get into another argument during the ball. She turned to Olav.

"Prince Olav, may I present to you, Lochlann and Ciarán Allyn. They have been my closest friends since childhood. Their mother served as lady-in-waiting to mine."

Orla missed the tiny wince Ciarán gave at the word "*friends*" but Lochlann did not. He would speak to Ciarán later, but for now, he let it go and extended his hand to

Olav. Olav took it and they shook a hearty greeting.

"Prince Olav, it is a pleasure to meet you. You hail from Fadersogn if I am correct?" he asked.

"Ah, you know your kingdoms it seems," Olav said with cheer.

"Aye, Your Highness, I quite enjoy learning about the kingdoms we trade with on our journeys. I have visited your kingdom and was enchanted by it. The mountains are covered in snow year round, are they not?" Lochlann asked.

Olav nodded and turned to Orla. "Princess Orla, would you think it rude if I were to steal away your friend for a while? I think we might take some refreshment?"

Orla smiled. "Not at all, Prince Olav. Thank you for the dancing. I look forward to speaking with you more during your stay."

Ciarán watched the exchange with no small amount of jealousy. Orla and Olav seemed like they were already quite close. He was sure an engagement would be announced soon. He was jolted out of his morose thoughts by Lochlann nudging him gently.

"You will be okay?" Lochlann asked under his breath.

Ciarán huffed and whispered, "Go, I'm not a child."

Lochlann looked between Ciarán and Orla and smiled as he followed Olav to the banquet room. The two of them stood in silence, neither willing to break it.

"Should you be here?" Orla finally asked.

Ciarán stiffened, giving her a cold stare. Of course he shouldn't but he didn't really expect her to make him leave. It only cemented his thoughts on her *"friends"* comment.

"I only meant...." she tried to explain.

"With all due respect, Your Highness," he interrupted. "I will return to my rooms at once."

Ciarán bowed again stiffly and steeled himself for the painful walk back. It would be more difficult without Lochlann to lean on. Orla followed him out into the hall, unwilling to let the matter drop.

"Could you just wait?" she demanded.

"Why? You have made it quite clear where my place is, Your Highness. I will return to my rooms, and you may return to your guests." He bowed again and walked away as quickly as he could.

Orla fought the tears threatening to come and squared her shoulders. She painted on her best smile and returned to the ballroom with only a fleeting glance back at Ciarán's retreating figure. She'd wanted to make sure he was better and she had only made it worse. She cursed herself for lack of eloquence when it came to speaking to him.

During the week Olav stayed in Eiremor, he and Lochlann became best friends. He was a very astute man and two things became clear to him in a very short time. Lochlann would one day lead Eiremor's Armada and the Princess was in love with Ciarán. He could tell there was some tension between the two, perhaps because they were too stubborn to talk to each other openly.

Granted, Ciarán's mobility was very limited and he mainly kept to his rooms, resting, but when he did enter a room where Orla was, her entire focus was on him. She watched every move Ciarán made and Olav saw the anguish on her face whenever Ciarán showed any sign of physical distress. Her fingers clenched and she moved to help, but then a look of resolve settled on her face instead and she refocused her attention on something else until he moved again. It was a delicate balancing act.

Olav and Lochlann were sparring in the courtyard. Lochlann was a very good swordsman and the men appeared to be equals. They were not really keeping score, but if they had, it would be about even anyway. Olav had not met any in his kingdom who could keep up with him. He'd just disarmed Lochlann, who conceded the match, and they were taking a water break while leaning against a wall.

"Lochlann, might I ask you a question?" Olav asked.

"Of course, Your Highness," Lochlann replied.

"Olav, please. You have earned the right, my friend. If I may call you that."

"Of course you may. Very well, Olav, what curiosity might I settle?" Lochlann asked with a smile.

"The Princess, she has an affection for your brother, does she not?" he asked.

Lochlann thought for a moment. He was not sure if it was his place to discuss Orla's thoughts or affections for anyone. She had not spoken to him of the matter but he was not blind either. However, Olav was a kind person and would one day be King of his own kingdom. He did not believe the question was born of any malice but rather a genuine curiosity. Lochlann did not think Olav would use the information against her.

"I believe she does but I am not certain of it. Those two fight more often than not," he said and chuckled.

"Ah, a passion born of fire. I have seen it before, my own parents have been known to awaken the whole kingdom with their shouting. My mother once threw a vase at my father's head during dinner, then sat back down and calmly ate the rest of her food as if it were a normal evening." Olav laughed heartily. "How does your brother feel?"

"Just as I am not certain of Orla's feelings, I cannot give words to my brother's feelings for her. Love is not strong enough for what he feels. She is his world. Whenever they are apart, he thinks only of her. Their most recent argument has wounded him more than the fall. He is just too stubborn to admit it."

Olav scratched his chin. "What is the problem?"

"Ciarán has grand ideas about royalty and he has always belabored the fact that he is not noble. Therefore, in his mind, he is below her station and not a suitable match.

Their recent argument did not help to dispel that myth when Orla pulled rank on him," Lochlann replied.

Olav thought for a moment, a sly grin slipped across his face. He had a reputation for meddling in the affairs of other and this would be no exception.

"The accident was not so much an accident?" he asked.

Lochlann laughed. "Very clever deduction. They were arguing on the wall and Ciarán might have been given a little push. How did you guess?"

"I can see the guilt written on the Princess' face whenever it is mentioned."

"Aye, she was never good at hiding her emotions," Lochlann said. He was really beginning to enjoy his new friend. "I do hope that my brother's affections for the Princess will not cause problems between our kingdoms?"

Olav grinned. "My dear, Lochlann, why would you worry about such things?"

Lochlann shrugged. "I just assumed you were here to try to win her over?"

"'Tis true that my mother and father would like for me to find a match and they are very fond of your sovereigns. However, I do believe that the Princess and I would make better allies than lovers. Would you not agree?" Olav assessed Lochlann.

Lochlann nodded. "Aye, I am not sure I would want to be the one in the way of what Orla wanted."

"I have an idea, if you are game?" Olav said conspiratorially.

Lochlann nodded. "Anything that would help resolve this situation. I can't stand my brother's moroseness any longer. What did you have in mind?"

"Lochlann, I'm not in the mood. My head hurts today. My

chest feels like it will collapse and kill me at any moment."

Ciarán whined as his brother pushed him outside. He wanted to stay in his rooms and sleep. If he was asleep, then he could not think, and if he could not think, his heart would not hurt. Olav and Orla had been spending so much time together. Ciarán could not bear to see her happy with another while he was so miserable.

"I don't care how much you hurt, you need some fresh air and I am tired of seeing you mope around. You are so pale that you blind me when I look you."

"That isn't funny and I do not mope," Ciarán huffed, trying to cross his arms and wincing at the pain.

Lochlann scoffed and stared at his brother, trying to hold in a laugh. Ciarán was acting like a child and it amused him.

"Fine," Ciarán relented and gestured for Lochlann to lead the way.

The brothers walked towards the meadow and Ciarán stopped short when he saw Olav and Orla sitting near the willow tree. Lochlann looked back and saw Ciarán turning to go.

"Lochlann, no. I can't," Ciarán protested.

"You can and you will," he hissed.

He grabbed his brother's arm, spinning him around and practically dragging him towards the tree.

"Ah, Lochlann and Ciarán, so nice to see you this fine afternoon," Olav said pleasantly.

Orla looked at the brothers. When she met Ciarán's stormy gaze, she looked away quickly, feigning interest in the stream.

"I was just telling Ciarán he needed some air and sun," Lochlann said.

"Yes, yes, a fine day for it. Wouldn't you agree, Princess?" Olav said.

"Yes, it is lovely today," Orla muttered, not addressing anyone in particular.

Ciarán stepped back, attempting to leave. "I think I have had enough air."

He bowed and began walking back towards the castle as fast as he could without too much pain. Lochlann glanced at Olav who nodded. He chased after his brother.

"Ciarán," he said in a low tone.

Ciarán stopped, waiting for his brother. He kept his back to the tree and the couple beside it.

"We are interrupting," he said in a whisper.

Lochlann sighed, looking to the heavens for help. This drama would be the death of him.

"Look, you need to talk to her," he said.

Ciarán shook his head. "She made it quite clear I don't. Olav is attempting to woo her, we should not be interrupting."

"Ciarán, I love you, but sometimes you are a dolt. You were both angry that day and the argument blew out of proportion. Harsh words are often said but not meant. We cannot take them back, but we can soothe the hurt they wrought. We can forgive. Besides, you have yet to give her a birthday present. That is very bad form."

Incredulous eyes turned to Lochlann. "Are you daft? A birthday present from me is the last thing she needs."

Lochlann pulled the small package from his pocket. Ciarán had wrapped it in a small scrap of green silk Queen Meara gave him. It was tied with a silver ribbon in an elaborate bow. His perfectionist tendencies meant he'd spent hours making it just right.

"Lochlann, just keep it. She won't want it," Ciarán said. "Besides, she and Olav seem quite close and I don't want to jeopardize her future. He is much more suitable for her."

Lochlann sighed. "Olav brought her out here so the two of you could talk, you idiot!"

Ciarán's eyes widened. "What?"

"Anyone with eyes can see you care for each other. He does not want to court her, merely earn her trust as an ally so that our kingdoms may be strengthened in mutual harmony. You have both been miserable this week. Look, just talk to her and give her the gift. Then you can go back to hiding in your rooms," Lochlann said.

He put the gift into Ciarán's hands and spun him around. He gave him a small, but not painful, push towards where Orla and Olav were waiting. It was clear Orla was doing her best to make polite conversation and ignore the brothers, but Olav could tell she was yet again distracted by her concern for Ciarán.

"Princess, would you mind if I sparred with Lochlann? He is quite remarkable and the best sparring partner I have had in a very long time. My father's guard are all getting old and slow. I am sure Ciarán might keep you company," Olav said.

Orla tried to hide her nerves at the thought of being alone with Ciarán. Things had been so strained between them and she had not been able to say anything right when he was around. She pasted on a smile as best she could. She refused to show weakness.

"Of course, Olav. Thank you for the most excellent conversation this afternoon," she said politely.

Olav and Lochlann both bowed and took their leave. They walked through the meadow towards the castle and looked back once they were near the door. Ciarán had not retreated yet, a very good sign. They shared a high five before entering for their sparring session.

Orla sat staring at Ciarán while he stared at the water. He had yet to sit but he wasn't sure he wanted to do so knowing it would be difficult to get up if she asked him to leave. He would not embarrass himself any further in front of her. She cleared her throat to get his attention. Slowly, he turned towards her and gave a small bow of his head.

"Would you like to sit?" she asked, patting the space next to her.

Ciarán took a deep breath. "Your Highness..."

"Please. Don't. I can't bear fighting with you any longer," Orla said.

"Very well." Ciarán bowed and turned to leave.

"Ciarán?" Orla entreated.

He turned back towards her. She struggled with what to say and he was ready to leave again when she found her voice.

"Please talk to me?" she asked. She patted the spot next to her again.

Ciarán nodded. He slowly sat down and found a position that was not too painful. He'd moved the wrapped package into his pocket and was careful not to mess it up as he sat.

"How have you been?" Orla asked after a tense silence.

"I am healing, Your Highness," he replied stiffly.

Orla looked at the paleness of his face and the dark circles beneath his eyes. She knew from the physicians he was healing, and it would take some time, but the pain was keeping him awake at night. He'd refused the sleeping draughts, claiming they made his head swim. She continually felt guilty and it affected her own sleep some nights. She would lie awake, longing to make it right, but unable to find a way to do so.

"I'm sorry," she said at last.

He looked at her suspiciously and his jaw dropped. Apologies from her were rare.

"I mean it. I'm sorry for everything. I shouldn't have scared everyone by trying to run away. I shouldn't have yelled at you for finding me and for caring about what might have happened to me. I shouldn't have pushed you, and I shouldn't have insinuated you were not my equal," she blurted out before she could help herself.

Ciarán scoffed. "That's just it, isn't it, though? I am not your equal and it was not my place to lecture you."

Orla jumped up. Ciarán attempted to rise, but found it excruciating, each movement shooting pain through his side and chest.

"Sit!" she said with authority, noticing his shoulders sag yet again.

"I didn't mean it that way!" she cried in consternation. She just couldn't say anything right.

"Aye, but you did," he said sadly.

Orla huffed. "Ciarán, I don't want to order you about. I want you to get well. This is all my fault. Don't you see that? I almost killed you!"

Ciarán laughed for the first time in a week, the sound foreign, even to himself. It might be better for him if he had died instead of suffering his current agony.

"It's not funny!" she failed to see the humor in it.

"Aye, but it is. I lost my balance and fell. You did not push me off the wall. I am mending, albeit slowly. You need not worry about being the murderer of a mere servant," Ciarán said bitterly.

Orla growled and stomped her foot. "Ciarán Allyn you are the most infuriating man I know. Why do you keep bringing up our stations? Why does it matter so much to you?"

"Because you are the bloody Princess and I am nobody. You have made that clear, Your Highness," he bit out.

"I don't care about all that. You know I don't. I was mad Ciarán. Mother and Father have both endlessly scolded me about being haughty and I did not listen. I hurt the person I care about the most in the whole world," Orla said as tears ran down her cheeks.

She plopped down next to him and buried her face in her arms. She had screwed everything up yet again.

"You don't mean it?" Ciarán asked uncertainly.

Orla sniffed and raised her head. "What?"

"You didn't come see me after I was awake but you say you care about me?"

"Of course I do, you idiot. I have been worried sick," she said.

Ciarán shook his head. "But only because I fell and might have died."

Orla rolled her eyes. "No."

Orla stared at him while he searched her face. He only

found love staring back at him and he slowly smiled in wonder.

"But Olav?" he asked in bewilderment.

"Has been a good friend. He has begged me to talk to you and relieve my angst, but you know me," she said.

"Aye, stubborn," Ciarán teased.

Orla nudged his arm gently. "Takes one to know one."

Ciarán nodded. He looked at the stream and thought a moment. He warred with himself about his next move, but Lochlann's nagging in his head finally won out.

"I haven't given you my birthday present," he said as he removed the small package from his pocket.

Orla took it and looked to him for reassurance that she could open it. He nodded and she unwrapped the package with care. She gasped when she saw the necklace. She recognized it immediately. Ciarán's mother was never without it and Orla always admired how much the pendant mirrored her eyes. Ciarán took her silence as an indication that she did not like it.

"It's foolish. I'm sure you got much better gifts at your ball... I could find something more suitable," he stammered as he reached to take it back.

"Don't you dare! It's my favorite gift. Your mother's necklace. Are you sure?" she asked and another tear fell.

Ciarán wiped away the tear and smiled. "Lochlann and I could not think of anyone else we would want to wear it. Mother said I would know who it belonged to and I know it is you."

Orla threw her arms around Ciarán and he tried to hide the wince as she hit his sore ribs. She felt it and drew back.

"Your ribs! I'm so sorry!" she said.

Ciarán shook his head. "No more apologies. I forgive you and I hope I am forgiven?"

Orla nodded. She looked down at the necklace.

"Would you help me put it on? I am never taking it off for the rest of my life," she said, holding it out to him.

"That's a big promise, Orla," Ciarán said. He put it

around her neck while she held her hair to the side. She turned back to him and reached up to lovingly stroke the pendant.

"I mean it, Ciarán." She placed a hand on his cheek and he closed his eyes.

In that moment, Orla softly placed her lips on his. Ciarán's eyes popped open wide. Ciarán felt as if his wildly beating heart would burst out of his chest. Orla smiled, resting her forehead against his.

"Thank you, Ciarán," she said and snuggled under his arm on his uninjured side.

"You are most welcome, my Princess," Ciarán said.

He closed his eyes and listened to the stream, content for the moment that Orla cherished his gift. He would have to thank Lochlann and Olav for helping him reconcile with her.

Lochlann shoved Ciarán in the direction of the King's study and Ciarán threw him a dirty look. He was getting tired of being pushed around by his older brother. Lochlann reached out his arm and pointed at the study door, the guards doing their best to hide their smirks at the antics of the two brothers. Ciarán took a deep breath and straightened his spine, knocking on the door. When he was granted entry, he gave one last pleading look at Lochlann who stood firmly, pointing at the room. Ciarán nodded and entered. Phelan was sitting at his desk reading some correspondence when Ciarán entered and bowed. He waited for the king to acknowledge him. Phelan looked up and smiled.

"Ah, Ciarán, to what do I owe this pleasure?" he asked jovially.

Ciarán stuttered. "Your Majesty, I would like... that is I

request... I mean..."

Phelan laughed and rose, going over to the side table and pouring a glass of water. He handed it to Ciarán, who drank it as if he were dying of thirst in the desert.

"Slow down or you will choke." Phelan took the glass. "Now, you have something to speak to me about?"

Ciarán nodded. Phelan waited but saw Ciarán pale. The latter was busy reminding himself that this was a horrible idea and damn Lochlann for pushing him.

Phelan sat Ciarán down across from him. "Whatever it is cannot be half as bad as you are making it out to be. I haven't seen you look this guilty since you replaced Orla's hair soap with honey when you were six."

Ciarán looked up with guilt.

"You were forgiven for that long ago," Phelan replied.

"Aye," Ciarán said. "You may have forgiven me but I am sure Her Highness still remembers."

Phelan laughed. "She very well might, she never forgets anything she might bring up as a weapon at a later date. But enough of this. What is it you wanted to speak to me about?"

Ciarán steadied himself and squeaked out, "I would like permission to court Orla."

"What?" Phelan asked, bemused.

Ciarán winced. He jumped up from the chair and bowed. "I am sorry, it was Lochlann's idea I should ask. I mean I wanted to ask, but I knew what your answer would be, and now, if you'll excuse me..." he stammered.

"Ciarán, wait. Lochlann is a very wise man," Phelan said.

"He is?"

It was Ciarán's turn to be confused.

"Aye, please have a seat," Phelan affirmed.

Ciarán returned to his chair, looking anywhere but at the King. Phelan studied him while he was distracted. Ciarán had grown into a fine young man and proven his loyalty to Orla. He had protected her for her own good and against her wishes, despite the physical pain it had brought him. She had not understood the implications of running off unescorted, but Ciarán's quick-thinking had saved her from a possible fate as a pirate slave or worse. Phelan could think of no suitor more worthy of his daughter. He cleared his throat and Ciarán looked up at him.

"Have you asked Orla if she might wish to be courted?" Phelan asked softly.

Ciarán shook his head and his shoulders fell. "No, I thought it best to ask you first. I am sure she would probably have laughed at the idea. A person of my low station should not have grand notions of courting a Royal Princess."

"Pfft," Phelan replied in a very, undignified manner. "Ciarán Allyn, of all the princes I have met from all the kingdoms, in my opinion, you are more suitable for my daughter than any other man. You are honest, trustworthy, and dignified. Best of all, you are not out to get her wealth, nor do you see her as a prize to be won."

"No, Your Majesty. She is not a prize. She deserves to be cherished and loved and respected."

Phelan slapped his knee and Ciarán jumped.

"Exactly. I know she would be in good hands with you. Meara loves her balls but if I have to meet one more snide prince come to court my daughter, I might retire to country life." He laughed at his joke.

Ciarán smiled cautiously and looked at the King with hope in his eyes.

"So, do I have your permission?" he asked.

"Aye, you have my permission," Phelan replied.

Ciarán jumped up and shook Phelan's hand, then remembered himself and bowed. Phelan laughed again and shooed him away.

"Go, tell her of your intentions," he said.

"Thank you, Your Majesty," Ciarán said and left the room.

"Well?" Lochlann asked as Ciarán swept past him.

"He said, 'yes,'" Ciarán called over his shoulder.

Under his breath Lochlann said. "Thank the Gods," and followed after his brother.

Ciarán and Orla spent as many waking moments as possible in each other's company. Orla was not disgusted at the idea of him as a suitor. Instead, she'd punched him on the arm and told him, *it's about time.* He'd blushed and scratched behind his ear until she kissed him on the cheek. That made him stammer and blush even more and she'd just laughed.

Since that day, Ciarán did everything he could to make her see how much he cared. He brought her flowers each morning in a little vase set next to her breakfast plate. They would stroll through the gardens, talking about everything and nothing, enjoying the unrestricted freedom they had in each other's company. In the evenings, they would watch the sun set into the ocean and name the colors they saw. They would spend hours in the meadow, Ciarán braiding flower crowns for her, or laying in the grass watching the clouds pass, naming the shapes they found.

Lochlann went about his duties in the Armada and received frequent letters from his brother. He was sure the next time he saw his brother, the news would be an engagement. Ciarán was recently given a commission as a Lieutenant and he wanted to propose to Orla before his first mission. Everything was falling into place for the Allyn brothers after years adrift in an uncertain future.

Ciarán asked permission of, Phelan and Meara to marry their daughter and it had been granted. He was making the final preparations to ask Orla to marry him when the unimaginable struck Eiremor. A neighboring kingdom declared war.

CHAPTER FIVE

Two weeks. It had been two weeks since Ciarán departed for Noregfjord with no word from him or her royal counterparts at his destination regarding his delay or his return. Orla tried to fill her days with tasks and busy work to avoid thinking not only about his absence, but also to keep herself from imagining worst case scenarios. Olav did not know if Ciarán made it there at all. He assured Orla that the rainy weather probably delayed the passage through the mountains, but she could not shake her concerns.

Presently, Orla was attempting to read a book in the library but not actually seeing the words. She stalled on the same page for hours as she stared out the window, not really even seeing the world beyond the panes of glass. She stroked the pendant around her neck—it had become her nervous habit over the years—and she was so distracted she barely registered the commotion coming from the hall. A great clang and shouting broke through her reverie.

"What on earth?" she mumbled to herself as she set aside her book, opened the double doors, and stepped into the hallway. Just then Quinn collided with her, he had not been watching where he was going.

She reached out to steady him and asked, "Quinn, what is going on out here?"

"Mother, it is Captain Allyn, he has returned and is ill but refusing help to his rooms," Quinn said in a rush, out of breath. The guard and Uncle Ciarán were fighting and he was searching for his Papa or Erik to come and help.

Orla's heart sank at those words and she hurried after her youngest son, who led her to where two of the King's guards were attempting to lead Ciarán forcefully towards the direction of his rooms, rather than the throne room he was insisting on visiting.

"Bloody well unhand me! I have orders to see the King upon my return!" Ciarán shouted.

"Captain Allyn," Orla said in her most regal voice.

All eyes turned towards her and Orla gasped. His face was deathly pale and his eyes so dark and sunken, he almost looked like a skeleton. He had only been gone for two weeks yet he'd noticeably lost weight. However, his eyes still lit up when they saw Orla. He made a stately bow and grinned at her.

"Yes, Your Majesty?" he asked with amusement.

"You. Are. Late." She punctuated each word in a deadly calm tone.

"Aye, Your Majesty. A regrettable offense for which I make no excuse but to say that first I was delayed by a storm and then by a matter of personal circumstances. I do apologize and am prepared to offer you a full report—" His words were cut off by a violent coughing fit leaving him swaying slightly on his feet as if dizzy.

Orla fought herself to keep from running to his side and holding him up by the sheer force of her will. She took a deep breath to calm her nerves.

"Captain Allyn, you will allow my guards to escort you

to your rooms forthwith. I will send along a warm bath and one of the court physicians to attend to you. I will personally inform my husband of your return. You are hereby relieved from duty for the remainder of the day."

Ciarán shook his head. "I do not need..."

"This is not up for discussion," Orla interrupted. "Guards, please escort the Captain to his rooms and make sure my orders are obeyed."

The guards bowed then proceeded to help Ciarán, whereby he promptly jerked away from them and hissed, "I can bloody well walk on my own."

Ciarán bowed facetiously and stomped away. The guards gave each other a look of dread before following after him.

Orla looked at Quinn who had been watching the proceedings with wide eyes. She put her hands on his shoulders and met his gaze.

"Go and tell your father the Captain has returned please."

Quinn nodded and ran off to deliver the news.

Orla made sure the bath and the physician were promptly sent to Ciarán's rooms. She also informed the physician that if he came back with a diagnosis of "allergies," he would be finding employment elsewhere and most likely not within the Kingdom of Fadersogn. He was to immediately report to her once a diagnosis was made. He gulped and went off to do her bidding.

She proceeded to the kitchens where she asked for a tray of Eiremor whiskey and Ciarán's favorite chocolates, to be sent to his rooms for his afternoon tea along with a selection of sandwiches and a lemon honey tea for his throat. Once done, she paced her sitting room impatiently waiting for the physician to find her and make his report. She itched to stand outside Ciarán's rooms but stood upon ceremony and waited.

After what felt like an eon, the physician was announced.

"Your Majesty," he said bowing before her.

"Do not waste my time," she said impatiently.

He nodded sagely. "It appears to be something with the lungs. We could try leeches to suck the poison from them but the Captain said, and I quote his exact words so I beg your pardon, 'I will not bloody sit here while you torture me with monstrous creatures, you daft idiot' and then he swiftly shooed me from his rooms with the threat of a cutlass in my back if he saw me again," the physician told her in an indignant tone.

"Is there anything to be done?" she asked hopefully.

The physician shook his head. "I have only seen this particular malady a handful of times and all with the same outcome. It does not appear to be contagious but generally affects blood relatives. At most, we can make him comfortable if he agrees. He is a stubborn man, Your Majesty, and he refused the potions I offered him. Perhaps you could persuade him?"

"Thank you, that will be all," Orla said, knowing that Ciarán would most likely refuse anything that might dull his senses. He'd hated those medicines when his ribs had been broken, and refused them for any injury since, declaring the pain was better than the headaches and nausea the medicines gave him.

She made it a point to compose herself as best as possible before she took herself to Ciarán's rooms. She figured he would have had enough time to bathe by now. She knocked lightly on the door and waited. She heard his cough through the door but could not discern any other sounds of movement. She knocked again and heard him bid her to enter. Ciarán was not in his sitting room, so she went through the open door to his bedchamber where she found him lying in his bed, propped against the pillows. He was bare-chested with the counterpane pulled up across his hips.

"Your Majesty, forgive me, I did not realize you would be visiting. Just let me get dressed and I will be with you momentarily," he said as he started to move.

Orla shook her head. "Rest, Ciarán."

"But it isn't..." he began, only to be cut off.

"For once would you listen to me?!" Orla shouted.

Ciarán jumped in shock and looked chagrined. He slumped back on the pillows. "Aye."

Orla cleared her throat and regained her composure. "Good. You will rest and stay in this bed until you are told, either by me or one of my physicians, that you are cleared to leave it. Is that understood?"

"Aye," he said again. "I apologize for the inconvenience, M'lady."

Orla choked on a sob, determined to not fall apart until she was safely back in her own bedchamber. "Ciarán, just stop. Please. You were never an inconvenience."

He nodded. "Would you perhaps talk to me until I fall asleep?"

Orla crossed the room and sat next to the bed. "Of course." She babbled on about nothing while he closed his eyes. He smiled at something she said but kept his eyes closed. She tried very hard to keep her speech soft and full of only light, happy things. He did not look like himself at all and her heart squeezed at the sounds of him trying to breathe without wheezing. After a while, his breathing evened out and the coughing stopped. She sat a moment longer, then exited quietly and ran to her rooms. She dismissed her maids and slumped against the door, sobbing into her arms.

Another week passed and Ciarán's condition did not improve at all. In fact, Orla swore it was getting worse and he was doing everything in his power to hide this truth from her. Olav suspended all non-essential council meetings and state visits, declaring the last vestiges of unusual summer-like weather too nice for them to all be cooped up over mundane matters.

The court, of course, knew that the Queen's most trusted and loyal friend was very ill. They loved their Queen and it pained them that she should suffer such a loss. They remembered a time when the Queen's father passed. She was depressed for weeks and the only thing to revive her was the discovery she was pregnant with her third child. The news had been so well received by her, she nearly glowed throughout the entire pregnancy and even after the child was born.

Orla was sitting in the garden with her children for afternoon tea. She felt as if she had been neglecting them these past days and welcomed the time spent with them in the fresh air. She'd even ordered the windows be thrown open in Ciarán's rooms and he be allowed to repose on the balcony instead of his bed. She fervently hoped it would somehow revive him and cure his ills. Surely sunshine and air would clear his lungs of their malady.

"Mother? Did you hear me?" Erik asked.

"Hmm?" Orla was still lost in thought but recovered from her reverie and met his eyes. "Yes? Actually, no. Could you please repeat what you said?"

"I was just asking what you thought of the new book that Master Lester has published?" Erik asked again.

Orla smiled at him. "I have not yet finished reading it. I started but had to attend to other matters." In truth, she had not been able to focus on anything but thoughts of Ciarán and was hard-pressed to care about her normal duties. She began it during his absence and it was the one she was attempting to read the day of his return.

Quinn spoke up. "Can we visit our uncle? How is he? Is he going to die?"

Erik swatted at the back of Quinn's head and Quinn stuck out his tongue. Erik rolled his eyes at his brother's bluntness.

"Oh yes, mother, perhaps it will cheer him up." Runa

agreed with an excited clap of her hands. She felt a small measure of guilt over the way their last conversation had gone. If her uncle died, he would have never known she did not really hate him.

Orla smiled at them. Ciarán had always been great with her children, somehow understanding what each of them needed when he was with them. He was patient and kind with her children, treating them as if they were his own. He'd never married or had children of his own and yet he had so much to offer a child. Erik, Runa, and Quinn often sought his company when he was not on duty and she knew it hurt them when she banned anyone but herself, the servants, and the physicians from his rooms.

She finally nodded, staving off their collective cheers with a raised hand.

"But one at a time. He tires easily and we want him to keep his strength to fight the illness and return to duty."

Orla missed the look Erik and Runa gave each other.

"Your Highness, it is very good to see you" Ciarán stated as he rose to bow to Erik.

Erik smiled and hugged Ciarán warmly. "Please sit, Uncle. You need to rest."

Ciarán chuckled. "So much like your mother."

"So I've been told on many an occasion. Mostly by you." He laughed.

Ciarán sat back in his chair as Erik sat across from him. "What brings you to visit a boring old man such as myself?"

Erik laughed outright. "You are far from boring. I just wanted to visit one of my favorite people. Plus, I do believe you have been missing our training sessions."

"Aye, I do apologize, Your Highness. I have been a bit preoccupied and your mother insists I not leave my rooms, though she has finally granted me leave to move about them as I see fit." He grinned and raised a conspiratorial eyebrow.

"Mother can be persuasive," Erik said and thought for a moment. "Perhaps we could find some other lessons here in your rooms. You have yet to teach me that chess move you use to beat me every time we play."

"Ah yes, I suppose sword fighting is out for now. However, chess would be an acceptable substitute."

"Can I speak frankly?" Erik asked.

Ciarán nodded. "Of course."

"We both know this is bad, do we not? By which I mean, your illness is not one from which you can recover?" he asked dejectedly.

Ciarán looked away, scratching behind his ear. He knew what the physician told him and he didn't need a diagnosis to know this disease would kill him, just as it had his mother.

"Aye," he whispered.

"Mother refuses to believe this. She has you resting so much because, in her mind, that is all you need to beat the ailment. We have not spoken to Father, but Runa and I wanted you to know."

Ciarán met Erik's eyes and Erik could see the sadness swimming in them. Ciarán did not want to hurt Orla but he knew his death would do just that.

"I know. I tried talking to her but she refuses to listen. She scoffs at the idea that she does not have enough power or money to change the outcome. She knows her magic cannot prevent death, but she swears the physicians just don't know that it can be cured. What else would you have me do?" Ciarán asked.

Erik bowed his head in thought, silence stretching out between them. He did not know what to do and hoped Ciarán would have the wisdom to find a better solution. Finally, he sighed and looked up at Ciarán.

"I don't have an answer. I just wanted you to be aware.

This limitation to her magic is frustrating to her."

Ciarán nodded in agreement, waiting for the younger man to get what was bothering him off his chest. Ciarán knew it was not only his mother's suffering bringing Erik to see him.

Erik looked away sheepishly. "There is one other thing."

Ciarán was patiently silent while Erik gathered his thoughts to continue. He could see the young man struggled with what he wanted to say.

"I am afraid—terrified really. I am afraid of being king after my father is gone. What if I am not a good king? What if my people despise me and I bring ruin to the kingdom?" he asked, his voice wavering.

"Erik, you will be a great king. You have your mother's spirit and your father's leadership abilities. I do not doubt you will be loved far and wide for being just and fair. It would have been my pleasure to have you as my monarch," he said with evident pride.

Erik did not miss the use of the past tense in Ciarán's speech and he lost the fight with his emotions. Ciarán was surprised to see the tears coursing down Erik's face and he reached out to lay a hand on the young man's arm. Erik rarely allowed himself these emotions in front of his Uncle.

"See, I am already weak," Erik said, swiping angrily at his cheeks.

Ciarán shook his head. "Crying is not a sign of weakness. It is strength. Always be strong and confident in your emotions. Trust them and let your heart guide you and you will be a king of legends. Denying them is what will lead you to ruin. Emotions make us human."

Erik laughed. "Thank you, Ciarán."

"It is my pleasure, Erik. Your father is a wise man and has prepared you very well to be the ruler of this kingdom. But do not worry, I have faith he has many more years left. He is healthy and strong."

"Do you ever regret any of your decisions? Do you regret being here instead of having a family of your own in

Eiremor?" Erik asked.

Ciarán thought for a moment. He struggled with the honest answer. He tried not to live in the past, it would do him no good now.

"Do you believe in destiny, Erik?"

Erik nodded. "I think so? I'm not sure. Mother once said she trained in prophecy magic but was not very good at it, so she asked to stop her training in that area."

"Ah, yes. You see, I believe she was actually exceptional at it, but often one does not wish to believe what they are seeing," Ciarán said.

"I don't understand," Erik said, confused.

Ciarán nodded. "Sometimes we might regret our decisions, but regret is not the right emotion. We cannot change the past, only affect the future. We learn from our mistakes and we pass that wisdom on. Suffice it to say, I do not regret having known you and your family. I have been pleased to serve you all. I will leave this life knowing I might have made even a tiny difference in your future self."

Erik's tears started again but this time he did not try to stop them. Ciarán was always the most selfless person and he had a way of making Erik feel good about himself.

"You should know that you did make a difference to me. My father was not the only person who prepared me to lead. I have learned many valuable lessons from you and I will make you proud."

Ciarán swallowed around a lump in his throat. "Aye. You already do every day."

They both rose and Erik once again hugged Ciarán, lingering a bit longer than normal.

He whispered, "I will miss you."

Ciarán hugged a little tighter, no longer trusting himself to speak without breaking into sobs.

chapter six

then

War was coming to the kingdom, and Ciarán had vowed to join his brother in protecting the Eiremor. The kingdom to the south had invaded the borders of both Eiremor and Fadersogn, declaring they owned the land south of the river. Centuries ago, the border dispute had been resolved peacefully, but the new ruler, King Johan, was a madman bent on world domination. Johan had run his kingdom into the ground and his people suffered. He promised them riches if they took up arms against their wealthy neighbors. The poor flocked to the cause and refugees poured in from the villages in the south with horror stories of the treatment being meted out in the wake of the starving army's progress.

Orla stood in shock, she had not expected the Armada to be mobilized so quickly. Ciarán was standing before her and telling her he was leaving within the hour. It was incomprehensible.

"It's too dangerous, Ciarán. I shall talk to my father and

you can stay behind. He can reassign you to some other ship or a castle guard position or something." Orla waved a dismissive hand and began to walk away from him.

"*No*! You will not!" Ciarán shouted and Orla stopped in her tracks. He'd rarely raised his voice at her, nor talked to her with such anger and venom—not since their fight on the wall. They'd both tried to move on from that day, forgiven but not really forgotten.

"Excuse me?" she asked incredulously.

Ciarán sighed and continued in a more reasonable, if not pleading, tone. "Your Highness... Orla... please, I am a Lieutenant in the Royal Armada and I have responsibilities to my Captain, to my Kingdom, and to my King. I cannot just give up everything I have worked for and run at the first sign of danger. It would be bad form and extreme cowardice. I have toiled long and hard to be respected and am now in that position of respect. What would people say?"

"I don't care what people say," Orla said stubbornly. "No good will come of this and I cannot let you go."

Ciarán nodded. "Aye, but you have that luxury, which I cannot afford. I must make my own way and do what is proper, and furthermore, what is right."

"You and that damn good form will get you killed!" Orla said desperately. "Ciarán please, we can change this," she pleaded. "I have seen it and I know it won't end well. I cannot bear it."

Ciarán scratched behind his ear and reached out a hand to lay on her arm. "Please understand that I must go. I cannot live my life based upon uncertain predictions. You chose not to continue your studies in prophecy magic, so you don't even know if what you see is true. If I do not go, people will not look kindly on me and it will reflect poorly on you. Your own father fought in a war when he was my age."

Orla twisted the pendant of her necklace in her fingers and looked him in the eyes, trying to hold back her tears.

She broke and wrapped her arms around him, squeezing tightly as if by the sheer force of her will she could keep him with her. He meant so much to her but she'd never told him the full depth of her feelings. He had to know even if she'd never voiced it.

Now he was going off to fight in an idiotic war that might keep him from her forever. She started to cry in earnest. Ciarán enveloped her in his arms and rested his cheek against her hair. He tried to soothe her, rubbing his hand on her back.

"I will come back, Orla. I promise I will come back," he said softly.

She shook her head. "You don't know that."

He chuckled. "Don't you know? I could go to the ends of the world and fall off the edge, and I would still come back to you. I probably shouldn't, but, I lo—"

Orla put her fingers on his mouth.

"Tell me when you come back," she said and he nodded.

Ciarán kissed her, pouring all his unspoken love into it. It was the first time he'd kissed her in such a manner and it left both of them breathless. He felt like he was drowning in her, unable to tell where he ended and she began. Finally, they were forced to stop for air. He rested his forehead against hers.

"I must go now. They're waiting." He untangled her arms and took a step back. He looked deeply into her eyes. "I will come back."

Orla nodded and composed herself, straightening a non-existent wrinkle in her dress. She took a deep breath and smiled. "Good speed, Lieutenant."

"Fair health and sunny skies, Your Highness," he bowed, kissed her hand, and winked at her, taking his leave.

ETERNAL WILLOW

Orla waited for three years. Three years from the time Ciarán promised her he would return, leaving her with hope for their future.

The war had been over for a year; her kingdom and their ally, the Kingdom of Fadersogn, finally defeated their enemy, but at great cost. So many lives were lost and she shuddered thinking about the price of freedom they'd won through those sacrifices. Their enemies used powerful magic in almost every battle and the defense drained the resources of both kingdoms. That was until her parents learned Orla and her younger brother, Kellan, could combine their powers and cast a protection spell over the two kingdoms and everyone who pledged allegiance to them. The spell proved so powerful, it decimated the enemy troops within their borders immediately by incinerating each person where he or she stood. After that, a hasty treaty was agreed upon and the war ended. But it had been too late for the majority of their enemies.

The resulting carnage from the use of their magic affected Orla and Kellan in different ways. Queen Meara kept her children's abilities secret from their subjects, but now they knew. She worried it would cause them to turn against her family, but most were so grateful they were saved from the carnage of Johan's army, they turned a blind eye and went back to their normal daily lives as much as possible.

Kellan swore he would never do such a deed again and only use his magic for good. He cried for weeks after casting the spell and the flowers would die as he passed them. Queen Meara worked tirelessly to help her youngest son cope with the trauma.

Orla was distraught at first, but was also old enough to understand she may have killed many of the enemy, but she also saved her people. She, too, vowed not to use her magic for such a purpose ever again. She prayed to the Gods daily for forgiveness. She felt punished when Ciarán did not return home immediately. The Gods had seen what she did and had not forgiven her, not yet. Orla tried to use her prophecy magic to find him, with no results. It was as if the protection spell had stripped the gift from her. She confided in her tutor, but he was no help, merely telling her *powerful magic has a price, my Princess.*

It was near the end of the war when news came of the Battle of the North Sea. Out of five ships in the battle, only one of the Armada's ships had been spared and returned to the kingdom. Orla heard of the returning ship and ran from the castle down through the town at breakneck speed towards the docks. She ran so fast, the townsfolk swore she was practically flying. She made it just as the ship was docking but stopped short when she saw the name, *The Mercury*. Orla's heart sank as she trudged back up the street and it took her three times as long to reach the castle as it had the docks. She waited for *The Mercury's* Captain to make his way to the castle and report to her father.

Orla was wearing a hole in the carpet when she heard a knock on the door. She opened it to find her mother on the other side.

"Mother, what news?" Orla asked.

"Let's sit down," Queen Meara said.

Orla shook her head. "No. No."

Queen Meara led her daughter over to a settee and pushed her down to sit. She sighed.

"The Battle of the North Sea was not kind to us, Orla. We lost four of our best ships. Orla..."

"No, the *Queen's Fortune* was not there. I would have known if it was there. I listened to the Armada's movements when Father discussed them with his councilors" Orla tried to deny what her mother was saying.

"Orla, the captain of *The Phoenix* took a direct hit and called for a replacement. Captain Lochlann Allyn's was the closest ship. The attack was sudden and Captain Allyn led the battle. Captain Smith has confirmed that the *Fortune* was lost. They pulled some survivors out of the water but most of the crew were taken hostage by the enemy ships. They don't know how many casualties there were before the ship sank." Meara grabbed her daughter's hand.

Orla yanked her hand back. "Then there is still hope. I refuse to give that up."

After the war ended, it had been agreed that all prisoners on both sides would be returned to their homes. In truth, their enemy was so afraid of the magic produced by the royal children of Eiremor, they agreed to every demand. They no longer had the manpower to continue the war anyway. It was now known far and wide that Eiremor would be best as an ally rather than an enemy.

The prisoners slowly trickled back home as they had been neglected in captivity and many still had unattended injuries. Most had been, at the very least, starved and were mere skeletons of their former selves. At the worst, they were missing limbs or blinded. As the days passed, Orla's patience began wearing thin. She felt the waiting was a personal punishment enacted upon her for being the solution to the war. She and Kellan both grieved at the loss of life from their magic. They knew it prevented even further loss, but it was still a heavy burden. The final group of prisoners, officers of rank, finally returned home and Orla was summoned to her father's council room.

Orla walked to the room with trepidation. Surely, if Ciarán had returned, the reunion would be much less formal. Her father and mother would have let him come to her immediately. She was sure of it. She just knew he would return. He promised.

She pushed opened the door and all eyes turned towards her. Phelan nodded and his councilors cleared the room as fast as they could. Their eagerness to leave had Orla's heart dropping to her stomach.

"Orla, please come in and sit down," her father told her.

Orla warily sat on a chair, perched as if she would flee at any moment.

"As you know, the last of the prisoners of war have been returned. Captain Allyn was among them and we have set aside rooms for his use. He is not well, Orla, but he asked to speak to you privately." Phelan told his daughter, watching her carefully.

"Ciarán?" she asked.

"We don't know," Phelan said with sadness.

Orla nodded. "I shall go speak with Captain Allyn, I am certain he will have an answer. Perhaps Ciarán is just delayed."

Orla left her father in search of Lochlann. She kept telling herself over and over again that she would know if Ciarán were gone. Surely he must just be missing and he would still return. If she repeated it enough times, she could make it true.

She found Lochlann and talked with him. It had been a very difficult conversation. He looked so fragile and shattered. Luckily he had not suffered any life-threatening injuries but he had a broken arm that had not been set properly, and Eiremor's physicians had to re-break it. He had been starved and beaten. He was lucky to be alive; not all of the ranking naval officers had been as fortunate.

Lochlann believed his brother perished in the attack. He could barely say the words, they pained him so much. They had gotten separated in the chaos and Ciarán was not in the group of captives Lochlann had been a part of. Seeing as Ciarán had not returned with *The Mercury,* and he, himself, was in the final group of prisoners of war to be returned, it was Lochlann's assumption that his brother was gone. Orla pleaded with him to reconsider and tried to convince him she would know if Ciarán were gone, but Lochlann could not be swayed. She'd fled from his rooms and refused to speak with him on the matter any further.

chapter seven

After supper one evening, Runa made her way to Ciarán's rooms. She knocked on the door gently in case he was sleeping. After a moment, he opened the door and smiled widely.

"Are you up for a chat, Uncle?" She asked.

"Always, my dear Princess," he replied and bowed as he opened the door wider.

She giggled and they made themselves comfortable. Runa reached into her pocket and brought out a small package.

"I brought you something," she said and handed him a handkerchief filled with a bright blue stone. "It is supposed to ward off pain but keep you from being woozy. I heard some gossip that you refused to take anything the physicians had recommended. I don't blame you, I hate those potions, they taste bloody awful."

Ciarán took the handkerchief and stone. "Language, Princess."

ETERNAL WILLOW

He waggled his eyebrows at her and she laughed.

"The vampires, they wanted to use leeches. It makes my skin crawl just thinking of it. Thank you, Runa. Your kindness and thoughtfulness is appreciated."

"Does it hurt much?" she asked as he coughed into his own handkerchief.

He shook his head. "Not too bad, I've had worse. It feels much the same as when I broke my ribs."

"Oh, I remember that story. Mother had been furious with you before she had met Papa and she pushed you off the wall into a cart." Runa clapped with excitement.

"Aye." He chuckled and started a new coughing fit. After recovering he said, "Your mother had a temper when she was your age. She still does."

Runa studied his fond smile and the glint it brought to his eyes, then she frowned.

"I'm sorry for what I said."

"It is already forgotten," Ciarán said.

Runa shook her head. "How? It was awful. I would have felt so bad if you had not returned and it would have been my fault!"

Ciarán chuckled. "Runa, always so dramatic. You did not cause this illness. I have already forgiven you. You are impulsive, just like your mother and I know you did not mean it."

"When you go, who will tell me of adventures and far off places? I had almost convinced Papa to let me go on a state visit with you as my escort. So who will take me now? Mother and Papa do not trust me to go with anyone else." She pouted at the train of her thoughts.

"Your parents love you, my Princess. They just want to keep you safe." He held up his hand before she could interrupt. "But shall I tell you a secret?"

Runa nodded her head enthusiastically. She loved her uncle's stories and was proud he would entrust her with something secret.

"You merely need to remind your mother she was once

young and full of yearning for adventure. You need to nudge her memory of her own obstinate denials of the desire to marry a prince and stay in a castle the rest of her life. She was quite insistent she was going to run away and become a pirate. She almost succeeded." He smiled affectionately at the memory.

Runa gasped. "She didn't? When?"

"Aye, she did. Got all the way to the tavern and was preparing to talk a merchant captain into smuggling her out of the kingdom," he said.

"What happened?"

"My brother and I found her before the pirates did." A look passed over his face but he shook it off and continued. "I went a little overboard in being her protector. So when we got back to the castle, we had an argument and she accidentally pushed me off the wall with her magic, breaking my ribs."

Runa laughed merrily. "*That* was why she pushed you off? You probably saved her from a terrible fate."

"Aye, but she believed I had condemned her to a life of mundane diplomacy. She also did not appreciate me insinuating I should protect her from herself."

"But Mother always said she felt horrible about that night because you were in so much pain afterwards," Runa stated.

Ciarán smiled. "Your mother's heart is pure and so she could not feel good about hurting me. She just did not think through the consequences of her actions. She learned a lesson that day and she never took her anger out in such a fashion ever again."

Runa nodded. "I see."

"Do you?" he asked.

"I believe so," Runa replied, "but I am not quite sure."

Ciarán nodded. "Remember this... there is a time and a place for everything. Explain to your parents that you know your responsibilities and you accept them but you would like to see the realms before you are of age to settle down and marry. They will appreciate both your sense of duty and thirst for adventure. You will most likely get what you want while reassuring them of your maturity."

Runa jumped up and hugged Ciarán, nearly knocking him over. "Thank you so much. You have always known how to get me to see things from a different perspective."

"I am always glad to help, dearest one. You are my favorite *niece*." Ciarán chuckled at her enthusiasm.

Runa pulled back and put her hands on her hips.

"I am the only girl, Uncle Ciarán!" she said indignantly.

"Aye, but it matters not for my feelings would be the same if you weren't." He winked at her.

Runa sniffed and he could see her body shaking. He tilted her chin and wiped away her tears.

"One other thing." He waited until she met his eyes. "Even when I am not physically here, I will always be here," he said, pointing to her heart.

She nodded her understanding and he cupped her cheeks in his hands and kissed her on the forehead. Runa threw her arms around his neck and he let her sob out her grief on his shoulder.

Ciarán was lost in thought as he stared out the window. He knew the children would be fine after he was gone, but it did not stop his sorrow at the grief they would feel. He did not know how he had let himself become such an integral part of their lives. He supposed it was a natural thing to happen when you lived in such close quarters.

He looked up as a knock sounded on his door. Before he could get up, Olav opened the door and walked in. Ciarán made to get up but Olav waved him away and sat down on the couch. He stared into the fire as he gathered his thoughts.

"Your brother was a fine man," Olav started.

Ciarán's brow furrowed. "Aye, he was the best I ever knew."

Olav cleared his throat. "He wanted you to be happy and I fear I may have dashed those hopes when I married Orla. He never said anything, but I knew he was disappointed."

"Your Majesty..." Ciarán began.

Olav interrupted, "Ciarán, just let me get through this."

Ciarán nodded and waited for him to continue.

"When I first met the two of you, I immediately felt as if Lochlann was a kindred spirit. I knew you and Orla had feelings for each other and I respected that. Of course, I thought she would be a fine queen, but it was clear to me you belonged together. That is why I persuaded Lochlann to follow my plans to help the two of you to reconcile."

Ciarán gaped at Olav.

Olav continued, "He didn't tell you?"

Ciarán looked away. "To tell you the truth, he told me you had helped him to plan the meeting by the tree that day but he did not say it was your idea. Now that I think on it, I can see where he would have agreed to it. Definitely something he would do and he would not have thought to intrude on your courtship on his own. I thought my feelings were one-sided and I was foolish to even dare dream she felt the same way about me. I was never worthy of her."

Olav laughed and Ciarán looked at him like he had grown two heads.

"Ciarán, in all my years, I have never met a more worthy man for any woman, let alone Orla."

Ciarán blushed at that and tried to hide his embarrassment behind a cough. Olav knew his friend too well not to notice but said nothing. They sat in silence for a long moment, each lost in thoughts of the past. Suddenly, Olav jumped up with a twinkle in his eyes and a huge grin on his face.

"Let's get out of here," he said, holding out his hand to

help Ciarán up.

"But I have orders to stay in my rooms," Ciarán replied as he stood.

"I am the King and my word is above all others. If I ask my friend to take a stroll with me, my word is law," Olav said proudly, puffing out his chest.

"She's not in the castle today, is she?" Ciarán laughed.

"No, she went into the village for a while with the children. Anything to get her out of the castle and give me a chance to sneak you away," Olav said sheepishly.

Ciarán and Olav laughed as they went out of the room.

They made their way out of the castle, through the gardens and up a small hill. From this vantage point you could see the village and the harbor beyond, bustling with activity. Ciarán missed having active work to do; it took his mind off both his illness and his situation in life. He had too much time to think lately. Sleep was his only escape, but now he had trouble sleeping in a reclined position and coughed too much if he lay flat.

Olav sat down with his back against the tree and gestured for Ciarán to do the same. Ciarán sat and picked at the grass next to him.

After some time, Olav spoke again.

"Do you ever wish that you could go back and correct past deeds?" Olav asked.

Ciarán shrugged. "Erik asked me almost that same question the other day."

"And what wise counsel did you give my oldest son?" he asked.

"Wishing would not make it true. It is a wasted endeavor. What's done is done. We must try to make the best of our future."

Olav studied Ciarán as the latter looked out at the village. He was trying to find malice in his friend but found only quiet acceptance of his fate.

"I suppose but I do wish some things might have been better. There are things I would change if I could."

Ciarán turned to look at him. "How so?"

"Lochlann. I would have wished that he were here now, to be with you as I cannot. You were very close with your brother and he would have been a comfort during your last days... I would wish that I had been a better friend," Olav said.

"You have been a good friend, Your Majesty. I could not have wished for a better one," Ciarán said sincerely.

Olav smiled but it did not quite reach his eyes.

"I have been jealous of you my entire marriage," he admitted.

Ciarán was startled at the sudden confession. He searched Olav's face for clues but found none. He could not fathom why this man, who had everything, would be jealous of him.

"But why? I am your humble servant. You are a king. There is nothing to be jealous of about my life," Ciarán said.

"Orla," was all Olav said, waiting for Ciarán to grasp his meaning.

Ciarán shook his head. "I don't understand."

"Orla loves you more than me." Olav held up his hand to prevent an interruption. "I have always known this – it was never a secret. When she thought you were lost, she never gave up on you until we convinced her to do so. She insisted she would know if you were dead. Her parents and I hated to see her suffering and I thought that one day I might be a suitable replacement in her heart. We wore her down until she was finally convinced to accept my proposal. I was very naïve. I am so sorry Ciarán."

"You do not need to apologize to me."

"I do. I am truly grateful that you did not fight for her, Ciarán. I am. But she was never mine and I should have been the stronger man. I should have released her."

Ciarán shook his head again. "The law would not allow it."

Olav shrugged. "Then we should have changed the laws. If I had not been such a coward, I could have persuaded my parents to change the laws for me as well."

"I don't understand, Olav." Ciarán was confused.

"I have never told this to anyone except Orla, Ciarán. I loved your brother, very much. I would have wished to rule with him by my side if I could, but the laws of my kingdom would not allow it, and I was not strong enough to fight my parents' wishes for me to marry Orla." Olav closed his eyes, fighting his emotions.

Ciarán's eyes grew wide. "Did... did Lochlann know?"

Olav nodded. "Aye. He told me to follow my heart and he would support my decisions. I fear I followed my head instead. You see, I am not jealous of you personally, Ciarán, I am jealous of the love you and Orla have for each other. I love her but not as much as I loved Lochlann. If I had followed my heart, I would have been able to rule with Lochlann and Orla would have been with you. Instead, my inaction kept all of us from true happiness and for that I am sorry. If only..." Olav trailed off, looking away.

Ciarán open and shut his mouth several times, trying to find the right words but nothing came out. He knew that Lochlann had cared for Olav deeply, he just did not know how much. Olav smiled sadly.

"I have spoken with the physicians, Ciarán. I know their prognosis and even if Orla refuses to believe it, I know they speak the truth. I have also sent word back to Eiremor and Kellan has created a tonic with his magic that will temporarily give you peace from your illness. It uses some of his nature magic that she does not possess. Orla continues to search for a magical cure but even she cannot change the rules regarding delaying death. It might help to give you more time to put your affairs in order. If you appear well, you will have more freedom. It might also help us prepare her for the inevitable." Olav fought back a lump in his throat.

"Thank you. I appreciate your concern for my well-being," Ciarán said sincerely and turned away again feeling awkward at all the recent attention.

"It is the least I could do. You would do the same for me if our roles were reversed."

"Olav, could I ask you a favor?"

Olav nodded. "Anything."

Ciarán took a deep breath.

"When I am gone, I want to be sent back to Eiremor. Orla will want me to be here but I don't want that. You have given me a place here, and for that I am grateful, but this is not my home. I wish to be near Lochlann."

Olav nodded. "I promise your wishes will be fulfilled. I will see to it, personally."

"Again, I thank you," Ciarán said.

"Think nothing of it." Olav smiled. "We should be getting back before she returns."

Ciarán chuckled and joked, "Olav, not afraid are you?"

"Absolutely not. She can't touch me. It is merely your safety I worry about," he said in a mocking tone.

"Aye, Your Majesty, I would definitely never hear the end of it, she would kill me with a look. Lead the way."

Olav clapped Ciarán on the back and they conversed lightheartedly on the way back to the castle. Olav locked the moment away, for although he had been jealous of the man, Ciarán had never faltered as an advisor or friend and he would be irreplaceable both on the council and in his private life. He would also mourn the loss of his closest link to Lochlann.

chapter eight

then

After the war, relations between Eiremor and Fadersogn had grown even stronger. Kellan and Orla had saved Fadersogn as much as Eiremor and the two kingdoms were now firm allies. Prince Olav was a frequent visitor as the official Ambassador of his kingdom and he and Orla would have lively debates over things as simple as whether you should have sugar or cream in your tea. She found him to be a pleasant man and they became good friends.

Her relationship with Lochlann was still strained, but she had seen him and Olav in deep discussion on numerous occasions. Their friendship had not wavered since their first meeting. Whenever she would come upon them, Lochlann would quickly make an excuse to exit and Olav would offer his arm for a stroll in the gardens or as an escort to whatever errand Orla was about.

Her life had slowly returned to a more peaceful state. Her duties returned to normal and she had garnered much more respect from the courtiers. She worried that they were afraid of her, but her mother assured her they were not. She still prayed to the Gods every night for Ciarán's return, but Olav helped her to feel more settled and kept her mind off of his absence. It was a year and a half after the war's end when her life was once again turned upside down.

"Orla," her mother said as she entered the council room.

"You wanted to speak with me?" Orla asked.

"Yes, Orla, your mother and I have called you here to ask you to consider a proposal from Prince Olav," Phelan said.

Orla shook her head. "I am not sure I can do that."

Phelan sighed. "It would be good for both kingdoms. You could..."

"What about what is good for me?" Orla yelled.

Meara shared a look with her husband. "Sweetheart, it is time that you accept that he is not coming back. I know it pains you, but Lieutenant Allyn is gone. Prince Olav cares for you a great deal and would give you a good home."

Orla stared in horror at her mother. "What about love? Do I not get what you have? Am I just destined to be married off for convenience? For politics?"

"He would not have wanted you to be alone the rest of your life, wasting it. In time, I am sure you will grow to love Olav as you did Ciarán," Phelan stated plainly.

Orla let a tear roll down her cheek. "It would never be the same, father. This was different, I know it. He promised he would come back."

Meara rushed to her side. "I know, sweetheart. We just want you to try to be happy and move on. To honor his memory by living a good life."

Orla shook her head. "I am not sure I can, but I will consider it, mother, for your sake."

She ran out of the room, not stopping until she could throw herself on her bed and sob away her misery. She cried for what seemed like hours-almost as much as she had cried when Lochlann had given up on his brother, after his return. A thought struck her and she ran off to look for Lochlann, who had recently returned from a mission and was waiting for his next assignment.

She found Lochlann sitting by the willow tree, staring into the water. She approached quietly and waited for him to notice her but he seemed lost in thought. She cleared her throat and he looked up with a startled expression.

Lochlann jumped up and bowed. "Your Highness, I apologize. I did not see you there."

"It is my fault, I did not want to startle you, but I see I did anyway. I wonder if I could have a moment of your time to speak with you."

"Of course, Your Highness, I am at your service," he replied.

Orla gestured for him to have a seat and sat next to him. She looked out at the water and remembered more peaceful times in this spot: all the times she had been here with Ciarán, laughing and planning for the future, and just relaxing. She rubbed her fingers lightly over the spot where he had carved their initials. It seemed to her that this tree was the keeper of her most cherished memories. It stood sentinel over her life.

"Olav has asked my parents permission to marry me," Orla said bitterly.

Lochlann stared at her, waiting for her to continue. When she did not, he said, "And?"

Orla whipped her head back at him incredulously. She thought Lochlann would take her side.

"And what? What about Ciarán?" she said indignantly.

Lochlann sighed. A mournful look crossed his face, the pain of his brother's death weighed heavily on him.

"Orla, you cannot mourn for him forever," he said. "At some point we must move on. He wouldn't have wanted us to wallow in misery over his loss."

Orla laughed bitterly. She poked his chest angrily.

"You are so quick to dismiss he is alive, but I know he is Lochlann. I can feel it in my heart. I would know if he were gone. I know I would."

Tears began streaming down her face. She huffed, so exhausted from her heart breaking she wanted it all to just end. She wanted to go back and speak to Ciarán differently. She wanted to be able to treasure every moment, now that she knew the outcome. She did not want to give up on him but she did not know how much more she could take. His disappearance was not something she could live with anymore. A piece of her was missing.

"May I speak frankly?" Lochlann asked tentatively.

Orla snorted. "More than you already have?"

Lochlann nodded humbly.

"Continue," she said primly with a wave of her hand.

"My brother was all I had left in the world. I did not want to give up on him either. But Orla? He would not want us to stop living just because he is gone. If we did, we might as well have died along with him. What kind of life is that? Olav is a good man. I could not ask for a better man to take my brother's place. Ciarán liked him and he would make a good match for you. He cares for you a great deal. If things were different, perhaps Olav would not be pursuing a marriage but I know that he will commit himself one hundred percent to being a good husband."

"But I do not love him, Lochlann," Orla whispered. "I mean, I love him as a friend, but he could never have my heart. I gave it to Ciarán, even if I never told him."

Lochlann reached out a hand and laid it on hers. He waited for her to look up at him and he gave her a sad smile.

"Olav knows this Orla. Affection as a friend is different. And yet he is still willing to give you a good home. You are fond of him, are you not?"

Orla nodded and looked away. She could see the truth in Lochlann's words but she did not want to surrender to them.

"Lochlann, what will become of us?" she asked.

"I know not, Orla. We must trust that the Gods have good paths lined up for us. We must look to the future and stop living in the past. I wish things could be different for all of us."

Lochlann sounded like he was trying to convince himself as much as her. Orla squeezed Lochlann's hand and looked back to the water, watching the ripples across the rocks while the sun slowly set over the meadow.

Olav found Orla sitting in the gardens. He bowed as he came near and she smiled and scooted over to make room for him on the bench.

"I was hoping I might speak with you on an important matter, Orla," he said nervously.

She smiled politely. "Of course, Olav. I think I might know what you wish to say."

"You do?" he asked.

"Aye, but please continue."

Olav nodded. "Orla, I was hoping you might do me the honor of becoming my wife."

Orla thought she had prepared herself for this moment but was unable to hide the sorrow and heartache that crossed her face. She tried to cover it as quickly as she could before Olav noticed, but failed. She summoned a smile and he smiled back timidly.

"Orla, I know your heart belongs to another." He put a finger on her lips when she began to protest. "I have always known and he was a good man. I know I cannot replace him in your heart. But I will love you as best I can and give you everything I can if you will agree to be my wife. You have become one of my best friends and I want to try to make you happy."

A single tear rolled down her cheek and he wiped it away. She slowly nodded in agreement. Lochlann was right, she needed to start living again.

"I will marry you, Olav," she said.

Olav grabbed her in a hug and whispered in her ear, "Thank you, Orla. You have made me the happiest man alive."

Orla insisted their wedding not be an elaborate one. Olav agreed. Both of their countries had suffered much during the war, and he, too, felt it best that they not overspend and flaunt their wealth when many had so little.

She was disappointed when Lochlann had declined her invitation. He had encouraged the match but he could not watch it happen. She feared their former close relationship was broken beyond repair. That day in the meadow, she finally forgave him for giving up on Ciarán, since she, too, was moving on. It was only fair but she had wanted to keep Lochlann close, since he was the last connection to Ciarán she had left.

Orla and Prince Olav had been married for a week and would be returning to Fadersogn in a few days. Although, customarily, she would have been married in his kingdom, Olav had agreed to have the wedding in Eiremor. They had also agreed they would wait to travel to Fadersogn, to give Orla an adjustment period as she was finding it very difficult to leave her family. Olav's parents had returned home after the wedding, afraid to be gone too long lest unrest happen in their kingdom. Their borders were safe at the moment but more volatile than those of Eiremor.

Orla had been reflecting on the past three years. How she imagined a much different life than the one she had been led to now. She had never dreamed she might one day leave her kingdom, although realistically she knew it must be. Kellan would be king when their mother and father were gone. She had always known on some level she would not stay unmarried forever, she just didn't let it sink in, denying it room in her head. She had imagined a day when she and Ciarán might be married and he could serve on Kellan's council. Then Orla could just be herself and not have the burden of ruling a kingdom. Not very grand aspirations for a princess, but she had longed for a quieter life.

She heard a commotion coming from the courtyard through the open balcony doors. She stepped out to see what was happening but could not make it out as the group moved towards the castle. She threw aside the embroidery she was working on and went to investigate. She almost collided with her mother on her way out. Meara recovered from the shock quickly and schooled her features.

"Orla, oh, I was just coming to speak with you. Perhaps you would like to walk with me in the gardens?" Meara asked.

"What was all that noise?" Orla asked suspiciously.

Meara looked away guiltily. "It was nothing, your father is seeing to it. Nothing that concerns you at all."

Orla looked into her mother's eyes, who was avoiding meeting hers. Meara had always been a poor liar.

"You're lying."

"We are just looking out for you, dear," Meara said and began to ramble, "This is just bad timing and if you give it time, everything will be okay. You will see. You need to go to your new home and get settled first. Captain Allyn should have given us a proper warning. He could have informed Olav of his findings and we could have determined a proper course of action.."

Orla paled at the name. If Lochlann was here, then he must have some important news. After he had declined her wedding invitation for *more important matters*, Orla had a fit of temper. It was not her finest moment and she had told him in no uncertain terms that if he did not attend, she would never speak to him again. She could not forget the pain she saw in his eyes as he bowed and left. He continued his duties with her father but stayed clear of her and the castle as much as possible during the wedding preparations.

When her temper had cooled, she could tell the reminders of her pending nuptials must have been like a slap in his face. Olav had confided his love for Lochlann to her. She had at first been shocked, but when she had reflected on the information, she realized she had seen Lochlann and Olav look at each other the way she and Ciarán looked at each other. Olav had told her how he and Lochlann had always discussed what they would do when she and Ciarán married. Olav would demand his father change the laws of the kingdom or he would renounce his claim to the throne and they would become privateers. Olav had decided to marry her instead of Lochlann and she realized it was too much for Lochlann to witness. First he had lost his brother and now the man with whom he had wanted to spend his life. If she had known before their marriage, she might have ended the engagement, but she would not embarrass Olav now that they were married.

She wanted to reconcile with Lochlann, but her pride kept her from reaching out to him. She suddenly felt selfish for barring him from a shared grief and giving him some understanding for the pain her marriage caused him. She had lost someone she loved but he had lost the only family he had. Lochlann Allyn adored his brother, and to lose him in such a manner, must have torn him apart.

"Orla, are you alright?" her mother asked worriedly.

Orla shook out of her reverie and stood taller.

"I will speak with Captain Allyn in my sitting room," she told her mother.

Meara shook her head. "Orla, I don't think..."

"Mother, I must speak to him. Please," Orla pleaded.

Meara studied her daughter for a moment and then

nodded her head.

"I will tell him and your father."

Orla took a deep breath and went to her sitting room. She sat as calmly as she could while waiting for him, attempting to prepare the right words in her head. After a short wait, he was led into the room, accompanied by both her mother and father. Captain Allyn bowed and sat when she asked him to do so.

"Captain Allyn," she started, laying a hand on his. "Lochlann, I feel I must apologize to you for my behavior the last time we spoke."

Lochlann's mouth dropped open. He shook his head.

"We all handle poor news in our own way, Your Highness. It was in bad form for me to refuse the honor of attending your wedding."

Orla smiled. "Please, let's dispense with the formalities. Call me Orla. I would wish to renew our friendship. I understand now why you declined the invitation and I apologize for my oversight."

Lochlann threw a worried look at her father and Orla looked between them. She did not miss her mother wringing her hands. They all seemed scared of their shadows and ready to run at any moment.

"Is there something else I am not being told?" she asked politely, looking back at Lochlann.

He nodded and looked to Phelan, who sighed, nodding his head for Lochlann to continue.

"Orla, I do not wish to pain you any further on the topic of my brother, however, I felt it my duty to inform you that I found him."

Orla suddenly felt dizzy and her mother rushed to her side. Surely this was a mistake, she had not heard him correctly. After a moment, she tried to regain her composure but seemed unable to find it.

"Excuse me, you *found* him?" she all but whispered.

Lochlann looked at her with sadness. "Aye. It was a stroke of luck but I have found him and brought him home."

"Is he... where did you... may I see him?" she was at a loss for the proper words.

"I am not sure that is wise," Phelan spoke up.

Lochlann nodded. "Orla, he is not wholly himself. I would not wish to distress you further. I merely wanted you to know that you were right and I apologize for ignoring your feelings."

Orla looked between the three people in the room with something between surprise and anger. She had heard almost nothing of what Lochlann said to her. Ciarán was alive, thank the Gods.

"I don't care what any of you think! It would *distress* me not to see him," she said bitterly.

She turned to Lochlann and tried to keep the begging from her voice. "Lochlann, please where is he?"

Lochlann sighed and scrubbed his face. He looked to Phelan for guidance, who took control.

"Captain Allyn, perhaps if we sent a carriage and some help, we could make the Lieutenant comfortable in his old rooms here? We have not changed them since he left."

This surprised Orla. Phelan and Meara had wanted her to move forward, but left Ciarán's rooms as they were. She guessed her parents had a harder time letting go than they had shown.

"Aye, Your Majesty, although my brother has specifically asked not to be brought here, I feel it would be most helpful if he were in a more familiar environment instead of the inn," Lochlann replied.

Orla watched their exchange with an eagle eye. She knew there was something else they were not telling her. A part of her did not know if she could handle any more surprises, but she had to know.

"What happened to him? Where was he?" she asked quietly. She watched as Meara and Phelan exchanged a look.

"Orla, sweetie, we will let you and Lochlann talk for a

moment while preparations are made for him to retrieve Ciarán," Meara said as they left the room.

After they were gone, Orla waited for Lochlann to continue. He walked over to the side table in her sitting room. He gestured at the wine and, when she nodded, he poured himself a generous drink. Orla could see his hand shaking as he took a healthy swig of the wine, then pressed his fingers into his eyes.

Lochlann cleared his throat and looked at her. "After we last spoke, I could not forget your words. Every time we argued on this subject, I, unfortunately, did not handle it well and drank myself into a stupor on more than one occasion. But the last time... the thought of no longer being your friend... the last connection to anyone who cared about Ciarán. I just could not stand it. I felt it was my duty to at least bring you some closure. To learn of my brother's exact fate, if I could, so you would be at peace. I tried, but every lead was a dead end."

"Lochlann, I am so sorry that I caused you so much pain when I should have been more sympathetic to your loss," Orla said sincerely.

Lochlann smiled and, with a little bow of his head, he continued.

"As you probably know, there have been pirates and slavers we have been dealing with off the shores of the kingdom since the end of the war. During my latest trip, we were attacked by a pirate ship off the south shore. It was a close battle, but I was able to get the upper hand on them, taking the ship and the crew into custody. I was inspecting the crew when one of my crewmen shouted for me from below. When I went below decks, there was a slave in shackles."

Orla gasped. "Ciarán!"

"Aye. I hardly recognized him. They had cut his hair and tortured him. They..."

Lochlann cleared his throat and looked away.

"They beat and cut him all over his body for sport. He

was malnourished and hardly himself. He did not believe that I was really there. It took much convincing for me to get him to come out of the hold and onto my ship. Even after he was safe, he slept on the floor." Lochlann choked on the lump in his throat.

"But he is alive, Lochlann."

She tried to comfort them both. She was finding it rather hard to focus and her corset felt entirely too tight. She remembered the breathing exercises her father had taught her during sword fighting lessons and that helped her regain composure.

He nodded. "That he is, thank the Gods. Apparently, he and two others had avoided being captured by the enemy during The Battle of the North Sea. But there was so much chaos, they had been skipped in the rescue. They floated on a makeshift raft for two days, waiting for help. When a ship finally approached, they flagged it down, realizing, too late, it was pirates. The pirates gave them an ultimatum, join them or die, and the other two were pressed into service. My brother, being the stubborn arse that he is, refused their demands and told them he would rather walk the plank. For some reason, this amused the captain and he decided to keep Ciarán as a pet. He had been chained and shackled below decks, only allowed in the light when it pleased the captain, and never allowed to leave the ship due to his big mouth. He has been a slave since the day he was plucked from the water."

Orla closed her eyes, the memory of Ciarán's sense of honor warring with her horror at his treatment. Of course, only he would be so stubborn as to remain a slave rather than becoming a pirate. Poor Ciarán. He had been a slave for so long.

"Let's go get him and bring him home, Lochlann," she said.

Lochlann took a moment. "There is one other thing, Orla."

Orla waited and thought she saw horror cross

Lochlann's face before he took a steadying breath. She did not think anything could make the situation worse. He fought with himself, attempting to find the right way to break the news.

"Just tell me!" Orla said, barely containing her impatience.

"He's... well..." Lochlann sat down, rubbing his temples. Orla's skin crawled as she waited. She could not imagine what could be so horrifying that Lochlann could not even bring himself to say it. Her leg bounced in anxious anticipation.

Lochlann looked up. He grabbed her hands and knelt in front of her at eye-level with her. He prepared himself for her to faint.

"Orla, they cut off his arm," Lochlann said.

After Orla recovered from the shock of Lochlann's final revelation, she immediately wanted to get Ciarán back to the castle. He had suffered enough. She'd wanted to accompany Lochlann but had been convinced to let him go alone. Her parents and Lochlann felt it would be easier for Ciarán if he did not have too many people around while he was moved. He would already object to it and if Orla were there, Lochlann worried that she and Ciarán might have a clash of wills, which would not help. Lochlann left with some of the house servants to fetch him to the castle.

If she were being honest with herself, she was relieved at the extra time she had been given before she saw Ciarán. As much as she wanted to see him, she also needed time to compose herself. She sought out Olav, who had been apprised of the situation by Phelan.

Olav knew the relationship Orla and Ciarán had before the war and how conflicted she must be, given she had agreed to marry him because she felt it was her only choice. Now that Ciarán had been found, he felt guilty for pressing her into marriage without proof of Ciarán's death. Olav promised Orla they could postpone their trip home if she needed to stay while her friend was recovering, but he worried she would dissolve their marriage now Ciarán had returned.

Orla knew Ciarán was now in the castle, having heard the carriage arrive, but she'd forced herself to wait patiently for word that he was ready to receive visitors. Olav asked if she wanted company, but she'd dismissed him, saying she needed time to think. He'd left after giving her a quick kiss on the forehead and squeezing her shoulder in solidarity.

She continued to wait for what seemed like hours when a servant informed her they were still making Lieutenant Allyn comfortable and what Lochlann had termed "presentable to her highness." She rolled her eyes in annoyance and sent the servant back to wait for further news. In truth, Ciarán could be wearing a potato sack with pink hair and she would not care. All she wanted to do was see him for her own eyes. To see he was indeed alive and safe and home. She stopped short at the thought of home, remembering that in a few days this would no longer be *her* home. She was in the middle of this musing when Lochlann, at last, knocked on the door and entered her sitting room.

He bowed low. "Your Highness, please forgive the delay."

"Please, Lochlann," she said with exasperation. "Just take me to him."

Lochlann scratched behind his ear. "He has asked that you not visit, Orla. I think we should honor his wishes."

Orla sighed. She knew this could not be easy for Lochlann, or Ciarán for that matter, but she had to see him. She had waited so long for his return and now he was so close.

"Lochlann, I need to see him. You must understand.

What if it were Olav? What if he had been missing for years and finally found and you were told you could not see him?"

Lochlann was not surprised at her insinuation of his relationship with Olav. He merely nodded and gestured for her to follow him. He knew it was unwise to continue stalling her. He had told Ciarán he would not be able to keep her away, but still his brother had protested until Lochlann felt he could delay the reunion no longer.

They walked through the castle to the door of Ciarán's rooms. Orla took a deep breath, attempting to steel herself for what she would see. She had waited for this moment for so long and prepared a million speeches, but now her mind raced and she could not think of one word.

"Are you sure?" Lochlann asked, giving her a final opportunity to change her mind.

She pushed past him into the room without knocking. Ciarán jumped, startled at the sudden intrusion, and his eyes widened. Orla stopped short, her mouth agape. He struggled to stand and Lochlann was at his side in a moment to help, fussing over his brother like a mother hen. This brought Orla out of her momentary shock and she regained her composure.

"Please don't get up," she said quietly.

Ciarán gave a short bow but remained stubbornly standing, leaning on his brother and avoiding her eyes.

Orla threw up her hands. "Oh for heaven's sake." She stomped over and plopped into a chair.

Ciarán chuckled as best he could and then Lochlann helped him to sit again. He patted Ciarán on the shoulder and the latter looked at him with fear in his eyes. Lochlann did not miss the look that Orla sent him and prepared to excuse himself.

"Brother, I will be near if you need me, just call," Lochlann said and waited for confirmation. After a moment, Ciarán gulped and nodded.

Orla stared at Ciarán, looking over him as much as she

could, taking it all in. He avoided her gaze, staring at her hands and watching them slowly twist into fists in her skirts. It pained her to see him this way. He was gaunt and tired looking, he must have lost half of his previous body weight. An angry red scar crossed his face, cutting through his eye, extending from his eyebrow and down to his right cheek. His normally neat, long hair was lopped off haphazardly and bare in places. She could see spots that were cleaned but scabbed over where the razor must have cut his scalp. His normally clean shaven chin and jaw were covered in a light scruff, which housed more scabs, probably because it would have been too painful for him to fully shave. She tried desperately not to notice the deep purple bruises under his eyes. Those same haunted eyes that now looked up at her both with trepidation and shame. She let herself linger there for a moment before glancing briefly at his left arm, his sleeve ending where his forearm should be but was not. He made a self-conscious move to place his arm between himself and the chair.

"Please, don't," Orla said in a whisper.

"Your Highness, I—" Ciarán began to apologize.

"Ciarán, there is no need for formalities. Nothing has changed between us," she said.

He looked pointedly at her left hand and she swallowed heavily, suddenly feeling too warm for the room.

"This does not change the fact that we are dear friends," she said.

"Friends," he muttered under his breath and she wished she could erase the look of hurt that crossed his features.

She moved from her position to kneel beside him. He started to rise again and she pushed on his leg to keep him seated, wincing with him when she must have hit yet another sore spot she could not see. She wondered how much of him hurt and where.

"Ciarán, what did they do to you?" she asked solemnly.

He laughed humorlessly. "Enough. I do apologize for

my late return."

"It matters not. You are back and that is what is important. You kept your promise," Orla said.

He looked down into her eyes. She was so beautiful and he could hardly believe that she was here in front of him. He had longed to see her face again.

"Aye, Orla. I am sorry it took me so long to come home. I was delayed by unforeseen circumstances. I am told congratulations are in order," he said earnestly.

He gave her a weak smile and that was what broke her composure. Orla threw her arms around his neck and started sobbing, her tears staining his shirt where she laid her head.

"Oh, Ciarán."

He wrapped his uninjured arm around her and let her cry for both of them.

Phelan and Meara hugged Orla as she prepared to leave for her new home. Kellan gave her a light-hearted punch on the shoulder, and she ruffled his hair like she had done when he was shorter than her. He threw caution to the wind and hugged her tightly. Olav was at her side and Phelan reached out to shake his hand.

"Take care of our girl," Phelan said.

"I will, Your Majesty," Olav said as he bowed.

Phelan waved him off and surrounded him in a bear hug. "None of that, we are family now."

They laughed. Meara wiped a tear from her eye and hugged Olav, followed by a handshake from Kellan.

Olav opened the carriage door for Orla and she took his hand to step up when she noticed Lochlann and Ciarán at the far end of the courtyard, watching the proceedings. She briefly looked at Olav and he followed her eyes. He nodded and she walked off towards the brothers.

Both men bowed at her approach. Ciarán was slowly becoming more himself, although she knew that he still experienced a great deal of pain. He hid it gallantly. She held out her hand to Lochlann and he took it, kissing the top in a formal fashion.

"We will miss you, Your Highness," he said.

"And I, you, Lochlann. Thank you for being a friend to me even when I did not return the favor."

"Think nothing of it," he said genuinely.

She smiled at him and then gave him a hug, which surprised him. She whispered in his ear.

"Take care of him for me."

Lochlann nodded and squeezed her a little harder.

Orla turned to Ciarán and smiled. Lochlann cleared his throat.

"I'd like to say goodbye to Olav, excuse me." He left rather quickly.

Ciarán shyly scratched behind his ear.

"Orla..."

"Ciarán..."

They both spoke at the same time and it helped lessen the tension. They laughed and Ciarán gestured for her to continue.

"Ciarán, please write to me and tell me of your progress?"

He nodded.

"Aye. I expect to be right as rain in no time. Orla..."

Orla waited for him to continue, and when he did not, she gave out a little huff. He chuckled and reached out to place a stray hair behind her ear.

"Well?" she asked.

"I forgot what I was going to say," he said smoothly.

"Liar," she said. "Tell me."

Ciarán smiled and gave her another bow. Orla lightly tapped him on the chest, still unsure where she could touch him and where he was not yet healed.

"Thank you for all you have done for me and for my brother," he said.

Orla shook her head.

"I have done nothing. And that is not what you were going to say," she pouted.

"Aye, it was," he replied. "Have a spectacular life, my Princess. Olav is a very lucky man."

She dropped the subject, knowing he would not tell her what he had planned to say. With that, Ciarán bowed one last time and offered his arm. Orla took it and walked with him back to Olav and the waiting carriage. Orla could see a lingering anguish on Olav's features before Lochlann surrounded him in a bear hug. Olav and Lochlann patted each other on the back and reverted to joking as Ciarán and Orla approached.

Ciarán gave her hand to Olav and stepped back. Olav shook Ciarán's hand in return, wishing him well, and helped Orla into the carriage. He gave a final lingering look to Lochlann, nodded, then sat in the carriage and signaled the driver to proceed. Everyone assembled waved as the couple rode out of the courtyard, Orla waving wildly as long as she could see them.

After they had ridden a short way, Orla asked to stop so she could take in her home one last time. She looked back and saw the castle, bathed in sunlight. There was the silhouette of a lone figure standing on the battlements. Ciarán lifted his hand in goodbye and she waved back. She swiped a tear from her cheek, regained her composure and then nodded that she was ready to proceed.

chapter nine

Orla was singing and Olav smiled over at her as she arranged a handful of flowers on the sideboard in the breakfast room. Erik and Runa looked at each other in disbelief while Quinn picked unhappily at his eggs.

"Mother?" Erik inquired.

"Hmm?" she replied thoughtlessly.

"What is going on?" Runa blurted out.

Orla laughed.

"Nothing, my dears. It is a most pleasant day," she said.

She ruffled Quinn's hair and he scowled at her, fixing it.

"Do you not like your breakfast, Quinn?" she asked sweetly.

He shrugged. "I would prefer toast and jam, but father says I must eat my eggs first in order to grow healthy and strong."

Orla kissed the top of his head. "Your father is right, little one."

Quinn muttered, "I am not little."

Orla practically skipped out of the room. Erik and Runa looked to their father for an explanation.

"Captain Allyn is feeling better," he replied.

Erik began to argue. "But the physician said…"

Olav held up his hand.

"Children, the physician is correct. However, your Uncle Kellan and I have found a way to put off the inevitable."

"Father, do you think that is wise? Won't it just hurt mother more?" Runa asked.

"You want him to die!" Quinn's outburst made everyone at the table jump.

Runa shook her head. "Of course not, Quinn, but I don't want to see mother or Uncle Ciarán suffer any longer than necessary."

"Mother already thinks he will beat this illness," Erik said quietly.

Quinn, trying to fight back angry tears, yelled, "Perhaps he will! You don't know anything!"

Olav studied his children, each unique and precious to him. They were growing up so fast and he would miss them when they married and left for homes of their own. Erik and Runa were, indeed, becoming young adults, and Quinn would soon follow, but for now he was glad to have a few more years with his youngest son. He knew Quinn was not taking the news of Ciarán's illness any better than Orla was.

"Your mother needed more time to come to grips with this reality. I gave it to her and do not regret my decision. It will be easier for them both this way. They deserve it for all that they have endured. Do you understand?" Olav asked.

"Aye, father," they said in unison.

Erika and Runa knew their mother and Ciarán had been very close friends before the war. They also knew some of the torture he had suffered at the hands of pirates after the war, although they had never been told the full extent of his injuries. Children were naturally curious, and Ciarán had convinced Olav and Orla to let him tell them the truth of his missing arm, but that was as much as he shared.

Olav went back to his correspondence while Erik and Runa quietly discussed this development between themselves. Quinn scowled into his plate as tiny sparks played between the fingers of his left hand, hidden underneath the table.

Ciarán knocked softly on Orla's sitting room door. She had summoned him for the first time since his return from Noregfjord. He smiled at the freedom of being once more allowed to walk around the castle. Kellan's tonic did make him feel as if he were cured, although he knew that the effects were temporary and that eventually the symptoms of the illness would return. None of them knew how long it would last. At the moment, he was grateful for the reprieve and took each day as if it were something to be cherished.

He smiled when Orla opened the door and gave a bow, to which she half-giggled. He raised an eyebrow but said nothing. He was glad to see she was in a better mood.

"Captain Allyn, please come in. It is nice to see you so well," she said, opening the door wider for him to move past her.

Ciarán walked into the room, noting several vases of fall flowers scattered about. He waited for Orla to seat herself on a couch and then took a seat in the chair across from her. She fidgeted, and he could tell that she had something she wanted to say but didn't know how to broach the subject.

"Your Majesty? Is there something you would like to discuss with me?" he prompted.

"Aye but I think I would rather show you," she smiled mischievously. "Are you well enough for a ride?"

That was music to Ciarán's ears. A chance to leave the castle and feel the wind on his face would be like heaven after being cooped up for so long. Since his return from the war, he'd been restless, never quite relaxing when there was nothing to do. He jumped at this chance.

"Absolutely, Your Majesty. Let me change into more appropriate riding clothing?" he asked.

Orla nodded. "I will meet you at the stables, Captain."

A short time later, Ciarán squinted into the sunlight as he walked from the castle to the stables. The days were getting shorter and soon winter would be upon them in earnest. He shivered slightly at the thought. His recent journey to Noregfjord was still fresh on his mind and that kingdom spent most of its year covered in snow. The cold had not improved, but rather worsened, his illness. He shook off the thoughts as Orla approached him, leading two horses already saddled and ready for their ride. She must have been very eager to get going.

He helped Orla mount her horse first, then mounted his as she held the reins steady. He prided himself on the fact that he had adapted to his disability and rarely needed help with mundane tasks. He could mount a horse without aid, thanks to Phelan. King Phelan, Lochlann, and many of the King's council members had taken it upon themselves to help Ciarán regain as much of his independence as possible. It took him a very long time master daily tasks without the use of two hands but not as long as it had taken them to convince him to try in the first place. He knew, however, Orla was enjoying helping him, so he did not remind her that he could handle it on his own.

"Where are we headed?" he asked.

She smiled. "You'll see."

She kicked her horse into a gallop. He shook his head and followed after her. He was not fond of surprises, especially when they came from Orla, but he decided to indulge her. They rode at a steady pace for thirty minutes and then slowed to a trot. It was peaceful on the country lane they found themselves taking, neither speaking, just enjoying the fresh air and tranquility.

"Ah, there it is," Orla said and pointed down another lane.

It led to a modest-sized country house with a rolling meadow that meandered down to a stream, not unlike the meadow of his childhood in Eiremor. Olav's parents had once lived in the house but now it was generally only used for prolonged visits from foreign dignitaries.

"Come on, let's go take a look," Orla said as she kicked her horse into a run.

Ciarán sat staring after her for a moment. He was trying to solve a puzzle for which he did not have all the pieces. He had visited this house before and it was odd to be visiting when no one was in residence. He went after her at a slower pace and she had already dismounted by the time he reached her side. She pulled her hat off her head and opened the door, waiting for him to follow.

They entered the manor and Ciarán looked around. It was a pleasant place, light filling the room from the long windows. He glanced to the right and saw a sitting room paneled in dark wood with a roaring fireplace. The furniture was upholstered in royal blue fabric and the tables were made of a rich, cherry wood. It seemed very welcoming. A servant entered from some unseen place and bowed to them.

"Your Majesty, tea has been prepared as instructed," he said.

"Excellent," she replied as she removed her gloves and handed both them and her hat to the servant. "Please have it brought into the sitting room."

She smiled at Ciarán again and gestured for him to enter the room. He was still very much confused and his face showed it. She just gestured again, so he rolled his eyes and went into the room. They settled themselves on the furniture and waited.

"Your Majesty?" he began.

Orla shook her head. "Just wait until tea is served."

Ciarán shrugged and tapped his fingers on his leg. He watched her carefully. Orla did love surprises. Perhaps she had bought this estate and wanted his approval? It seemed like an idyllic retreat and would be a wonderful place for the children to escape the castle. When she was younger, Orla had expressed her desires to live in a more proper home instead of *a drafty, miserable castle*. He chuckled at the memory but did not realize that it had been out loud until Orla looked at him like he was crazy.

"Just remembering something," he said by way of explanation.

She was about to reply when their tea and refreshments were brought into the room. Orla made herself busy putting everything in order and dismissing the servants. She began babbling about tea and what he might like to eat. Ciarán's patience with the mystery was wearing thin. She handed him his tea and sat down.

"Your Majesty, What is the purpose of our visit here?" he asked at last.

He raised a brow and took a sip of his tea.

"I wanted to personally bring you to visit your new home," she said.

Ciarán choked on the tea. He could not have heard her correctly. When he recovered, he felt a sense of impending dread.

"I beg your pardon?" he said.

"Ciarán, this is your new home. You deserve much more but I thought it would be nice for you to have your own place now that I have convinced Olav to allow you to retire."

"YOU DID WHAT?" he yelled.

He caught himself and clenched his jaw as he sat the teacup down. Orla raised her chin, a move he knew all too well. She was settling in for a battle of wills.

She said in a deadly calm voice, "You are to retire, Captain. You have served our kingdom and me faithfully for many years and have earned a rest."

"I do not wish to retire, Orla," he said with venom.

"Captain Allyn, you have served me well but I am your Queen."

Ciarán seethed at her pulling rank. It was a defense mechanism she pulled when she knew that she had done something she ought not to have done. It had caused many an argument and this would be no exception. He was so angry that he ignored protocol and stood, turning his back to her and running a hand through his hair. He turned back, hoping to make her see reason.

He tried to plead his case. "Your Majesty, I have always done all you ask, however, I do not wish to languish about and do nothing, in the country, away from you and your family. I don't need an estate, I would prefer to stay in the castle and be of service."

She bit her lip, trying a different tactic. "I took great pains to find a suitable place. This estate comes with a generous income that will serve you well. I want to give you something for all that you have given us."

Ciarán looked skyward, hoping the Gods would help him out. He took a deep breath and tried again.

"I have been quite happy with my current living arrangements and am still useful. I am not an invalid. I do not need to be put out to pasture."

"You almost *died*," she cried out. "I don't want you to feel like you owe us anything else. Certainly not your life. I want you to have a place you can call your own. You aren't far from the castle and the air is better here."

Ciarán had heard enough. He needed to get away from her. He stormed out the door, ignoring her demands that he return and finish the conversation. He stomped out of the house past the stunned servants, who had been listening in the hall, no doubt after his outburst had caught their attention. He made his way down to the stream they had seen and crouched down next to it. He picked up a pebble and skipped it across the water. Repeating the action, he tried to calm his racing mind.

He knew the tonic was temporary and it was both his and Olav's hopes that Orla would be able to see reason and come to grips with his imminent death. This was completely the opposite of their wishes. She continued to feign ignorance. On top of that, he felt like she was banishing him to the country, away from any chance of keeping his mind occupied during the last of his days. She would rather he die of boredom and didn't understand that it was a fate worse than his illness. He huffed and sat down on the bank, resting his chin on his knees.

Ciarán did not know how long he sat there mulling this new development before he heard her walking softly up behind him.

"Captain Allyn," she said but stopped when she saw his shoulders stiffen.

She placed a hand on his shoulder.

"Ciarán," she tried again.

"Aye?"

She took that as an invitation to sit down and arranged her riding skirt around her while dusting off imaginary lint. She hesitated for a moment, gathering her thoughts. He raised an eyebrow at her when she met his eyes. She smiled sadly.

"I'm sorry," she said.

Ciarán's shoulders relaxed and he shook his head.

"No, I mean it," she said. "I only wanted to protect you but instead I implied that you are not a capable man. Please know you are more than capable; I have never seen you as anything less. I just wanted you to be comfortable without working so much."

"I understand but don't you see, Orla. If I am sent away, then I might as well be dead." He stared at her and watched the tears pool in her eyes.

"Please don't say that," she whispered.

A tear made its way down her cheek and he absentmindedly reached out to wipe it away. He pulled his hand back when her eyes widened. He looked away, scratching behind his ear. They both stared at the water, lost in their own thoughts.

"This could never be my home. My home is with you," he confessed.

Orla bit her lip. "I've always worried if it has been a good home. Living with us. If, perhaps, you would not have been happier somewhere else."

Ciarán shook his head. "Never."

Light snow began to fall, the flakes drifting on top of the water. Ciarán rose and helped Orla stand. They made their way back to the horses at the manor and rode towards the castle. When they arrived at the stables, the snowfall had become a little heavier. Ciarán helped Orla dismount and went to take care of the horses but before he left, Orla stopped him.

"Captain Allyn?" she asked, returning to formality.

He looked back at her.

"I should have realized this was a bad idea. Please forgive me?" she said.

Ciarán bowed and turned away to return the horses to the stables. When he had finished, the entire courtyard was covered in a light blanket of snow. He stood in the middle of the courtyard with his eyes closed. The world stood still in that moment—the air smelled fresh, and there was almost no sound, the snow blotting out the world. He locked the moment away in his memories for he knew he would need the tranquility of this moment in days to come.

chapter ten

then

In the months after Orla's departure, Lochlann helped Ciarán slowly return to a normal life. It took a lot of trial and error in finding ways that he could do things for himself with only one hand. Lochlann put up with the angry outbursts and the sullen quiet with grace. He was so happy that his brother had been returned to him alive, if not in one piece, that he could endure his brother's moods.

Lochlann had convinced Ciarán to ride out on a hunt with King Phelan while he went about some minor errands in the village. He had just returned to the castle when a small retinue from Fadersogn rode in. Lochlann smiled and raised a hand in salute when he spotted Olav at the head of the group.

"Your Highness," Lochlann said as he bowed.

Olav laughed as he dismounted his horse. "Lochlann, my friend, what I have I told you of this nonsense."

Lochlann laughed, too, and the men shared a hearty handshake, each glad to see the other. The handshake turned into a warm hug and each one lingered for a moment, glad to see the other.

"What brings you to Eiremor this late in the season?" Lochlann inquired.

"My father had an urgent request for King Phelan. Our eastern borders are still unstable and he thought the King might be able to help us out. I offered to deliver the correspondence myself," Olav answered.

"And how fares your lovely wife?" Lochlann inquired.

"Ah, Orla." Olav sighed. "She is still finding it a bit hard to adjust to my kingdom and our court. She is so strong-willed, the other ladies are not sure what to make of it. She has been through four personal guards already."

Lochlann laughed. "Yes, that sounds like her. I doubt you will find anyone she approves of in that regard."

Olav nodded. "and Ciarán? Is he recovered?"

"He is adapting well. Just today, I convinced him to ride out on the hunt. The first time I have been able to get him out of the castle grounds since his return. Progress is slow, but thank the Gods there is progress." Lochlann smiled fondly.

"Your brother has endured much. It is a testament to his character that it did not drive him insane," Olav replied.

"Aye, Your Highness, I am very proud of him. Shall we go in and find some refreshment? I am sure the Queen will be happy for news of her daughter."

Olav nodded and followed Lochlann into the castle.

Ciarán swore at the horse. The hunters were finishing up their refreshments before heading back to the castle, and he was trying to mount the damn thing because it took him entirely too long to do so. He swore again as the horse stepped away from him. Lochlann had shown him countless times how to do this task one-handed but the animal itself was not cooperating as if it, too, questioned his capabilities. He was on the verge of just giving up and walking back when he heard a voice behind him.

"It merely senses your consternation," Phelan said.

Ciarán bowed. "Your Majesty, I am trying my best, but the beast will not stay still."

"Aye, Ciarán, but you are telling the horse that you, yourself, do not believe you can ride it."

"I haven't said a word," he huffed.

Phelan took the reins. "Actions are sometimes louder than words, Ciarán. Horses are sensitive and can tell what we are thinking."

Phelan stroked the horse's neck, talking gibberish to it. After a minute, the horse calmed and did not shy away from Ciarán. Ciarán sighed in relief. Phelan looked back at him.

"See, you just have to let it know you are capable of being in charge," he said.

"That's just it, I'm not capable," Ciarán muttered.

Phelan put his hands on Ciarán's shoulders and looked into his eyes.

"Ciarán Allyn, you need to stop feeling sorry for yourself. Life does not always happen the way we think it should, but you are alive. It is far better than being dead. Your brother was not the same man when he thought you were gone. You might not believe it, but you are loved, and when we thought you had died in that battle, we all grieved the loss. You are alive and well and resilient. Overcome this as you would any other hardship, I know you can."

Ciarán looked away and his cheeks turned red. He'd lost both his parents at such a young age and always believed himself dispensable. The sincerity of the King's speech left him with gratitude he did not know how to express. Phelan surprised him by embracing him in a tight hug. Then he looked at Ciarán and gave a little nod, handing the reins of the horse back to him. Ciarán took them and mounted the horse with one motion.

"Come, let's return home," Phelan said and Ciarán smiled.

A few days passed while Phelan made preparations to send some of the ships in Eiremor's Armada to the aid of Fadersogn. Olav would be taken home via ship, so Olav and Lochlann took up their old habit of sparring while he waited. They were fairly equally matched and Ciarán was watching them from his perch on the wall. They bantered and laughed as they fought, each trying to distract the other.

"Olav, quick, his left side is open!" Ciarán shouted jovially.

"Little brother, you are supposed to be on my side," Lochlann said as he quickly swatted at the sweat running into his eyes and tried to focus on Olav's attack.

"'Younger' brother, and just for that I remain firmly rooting for Olav," Ciarán said.

Olav chuckled and parried a swat aimed for his head. He spun and took advantage of Lochlann's still unprotected left side. The blow sent Lochlann into the dirt while Ciarán laughed heartily. Olav gave a silly bow in his direction. While he was distracted, Lochlann swatted him on the butt with his sword and Olav lost his balance and fell. Lochlann laughed and helped Olav up. Both men walked over and took a drink of water, leaning back against the wall.

Ciarán ribbed Lochlann. "You always did leave your left side open when you got cocky."

Lochlann raised an eyebrow. "Is that so? Well why don't you show me how it's done, little brother"

Ciarán's face fell. He clenched his jaw.

"You bloody well know I can't anymore," he said as he

stomped away.

Lochlann swore under his breath. "Ciarán, I'm sorry. I didn't think..."

But it was too late as Ciarán had already disappeared around the corner. Lochlann slammed his fist down on the wall.

"Lochlann, my friend, it was an innocent mistake," Olav said comfortingly, laying a hand on Lochlann's shoulder.

Lochlann sighed.

"He refuses to learn to fight again. I wish there was more I could do for him. He has been getting so much better at things, that I forget that he is a changed man. He is becoming bored now, but I just don't know what position he could take that would make him happy. He doesn't want to be a burden to anyone."

Olav nodded. "I take it that his disability no longer allows him to serve on a ship?"

"Aye, and Their Majesties gave him a pension for services rendered in the war. That was a miserable week. The realization that he was no longer fit for duty was harsh for him."

Lochlann rubbed his temples. Ciarán had ranted and raved about being *let out to pasture*. No matter how much Lochlann reminded him that it was an honorable discharge, Ciarán would not let himself be consoled. Later that night, Lochlann had tried to gallantly ignore the sobbing he heard from Ciarán's room. It pained him to see his brother continue suffering heartache after heartache.

"Lochlann, I think I might have just thought of a solution to the problem," Olav said suddenly.

"You have?" he asked.

"Indeed. You are to Captain one the ships heading to my kingdom, yes?" he inquired.

Lochlann nodded.

"Excellent. Let us talk with Their Majesties, I believe this plan will work." Olav smiled jovially.

Ciarán leaned over the railing of the ship as the castle in Fadersogn came into view. It sat overlooking a village of a considerable size. There were rolling hills around it and although it was somewhat late fall, the trees still held leaves of golden oranges and fiery reds. He could see snow in the distant mountains and the harbor was bustling with activity. The castle itself was much larger than the one in Eiremor.

He had been very surprised when King Phelan asked him if he would like to accompany Lochlann to return Olav to his home. Ciarán was to stay as a guest in the castle while the Armada continued on to the east to deal with the unrest. He had jumped at the opportunity to get away from Eiremor. It seemed that everyone he once knew barely hid their pity when looking at him. He did not want their pity and he was helpless to stop the anger that arose in him each time he caught the emotion in their eyes.

Olav joined him at the railing, glad to be home once again. "It is beautiful, is it not?" he asked.

Ciarán nodded.

Olav continued, "I wondered if I might have a word with you?"

"You may," Ciarán said and turned to look at Olav.

"I have taken the liberty of speaking with your brother, first. He informed me you have been retired from sea life?" Olav said.

Ciarán looked away and clenched his jaw. He took a steadying breath and turned back to the railing, gripping it hard. "Aye, Your Majesty. My disability is a hindrance and would put a crew in danger," he said bitterly.

Olav nodded. "I see. I was telling your brother that there is an open position in my kingdom for a man with skills and knowledge such as yours."

Ciarán looked at him in shock. He closed his mouth when he realized he had left it hanging open. What could he possibly do with only one hand?

"My... skills? I am not sure I understand," he stammered.

"It is my duty, upon marriage, to see that my wife, Her Royal Highness Orla, has a personal captain to guard her affairs and advise her. The captain would also be at my disposal, should I have need of him, to conduct business on my behalf. I have been unable to find a suitable captain for her. As you know, she has her own ideas about who would be worthy for the task."

Ciarán laughed. Yes, indeed, Orla had her own ideas on pretty much every subject imaginable. He could only guess at what she might have put a *guard* through, especially in a new kingdom with people who did not know her. The guards in Eiremor loved their Princess, but even they tended to volunteer, rather enthusiastically, for any task that would take them out of her path. Olav laughed too, he had seen firsthand what happened when Orla was set upon something against the counsel of her guards. Her last guard had gotten so fed up that he had decided serving the Gods was a better use of his time.

"As you might have already deduced, there is no one I have suggested who meets her standards. We have been through four already. However, Lochlann and I believe you have the unique qualifications for this position. That is if you would be willing to take it up?" Olav asked hopefully.

Ciarán thought for a moment. He did not know what would be worse. Seeing Orla every day but unable to be with her or never seeing her again. He had assumed, now that he was disfigured and scarred, that he would remain a bachelor his entire life. Did he want to be a bachelor in the company of the one woman he had loved his entire life while she, herself, was happily married with a family of her own?

The upside of the arrangement would be that he could

always ensure her safety. He would never have to wonder if she were hurt, or lonely, or sad. He would know and be in a position to help her as best he could. However, he didn't know if he could he leave Lochlann. His brother was returning to full-time service in the Armada, so he would be away at sea most of the time anyway. Perhaps they could see each other when the Armada visited Fadersogn.

Olav could see the war going on in Ciarán's head. In truth, he did not know if he would take the position, were he in Ciarán's shoes. Olav knew Ciarán loved Orla and had given her up for her sake, not his own. The day Ciarán returned from slavery, Olav had suggested to Lochlann that Orla might not want to stay with him now that his brother was back. Lochlann had smiled sadly and informed him Ciarán would walk to the ends of the earth for Orla but would never, ever besmirch her name. The law and society would not look kindly on her if she were to dissolve the marriage. Olav had dropped the matter but sighed in relief when Orla had finally agreed to set the date for returning to Fadersogn. Now, he believed that allowing Ciarán to serve as her captain would be good for everyone. It eased his guilt at having persuaded her to marry him with such poor timing.

"Your Highness?" Ciarán said at last. "I humbly accept your offer."

Olav shook his hand and went to make preparations to disembark the ship. Ciarán missed the thumbs up that he gave Lochlann on the way below deck. He was too busy looking out at the castle and worrying about the upcoming reunion with Orla. What would she think of this arrangement? Would she want a handicapped man appointed to the position, a constant reminder of the people they once were?

It turned out that Orla was ecstatic at the choice. She'd sorely missed Ciarán, and her entire being lit up at the unexpected surprise of his arrival. Olav hadn't had time to send word of the arrangements and decided it would be best if she heard it from his own lips. When Olav broached the subject, she could not stop smiling. She smiled so much that day, she thought her cheeks would break. Ciarán was taken back by the radiance of it. She could light up a room when she was happy, her magic causing her to practically glow. He bowed and she waved it off, giving him a fierce hug. He scratched behind his ear in embarrassment and she found it endearing. The gesture reminded her of home and all that was once familiar between them. Nothing would take away her excitement.

A suite of rooms was prepared for him, as befitting his new station and a ceremony was hastily put together to invest him before Lochlann was to leave. Orla pinned the badge of his station on him in front of Olav, his parents, and Lochlann. She said the proper words, but inside she was eagerly awaiting the moment when he would officially be her Captain and they could have a moment to speak alone. A special dinner was planned to mark the occasion and she bounced her foot throughout, impatiently wanting the meal to be over. She stole glances at him as much as she could, assessing his demeanor as he talked to Lochlann.

Dinner was completed and Olav went off with his father and Lochlann to make the final plans for departure. Olav's mother retired to her rooms, claiming she had a headache. Ciarán excused himself, bowed to Orla and started to return to his own rooms, the day's activities having exhausted him. Orla stopped him with a hand on his arm.

"Captain Allyn." She giggled at the title and he raised an eyebrow. She cleared her throat. "Might I have a private word with you regarding your duties?"

Ciarán bowed and followed her to her sitting rooms. The rooms had been decorated much like the ones she had in Eiremor. Some minor details were different but overall the effect was the same – home. He wondered if, in time, he too might be able to change the foreign rooms he was assigned into something familiar. He made a note to ask her about that later. He did not want to ask for too much, as being given this position was already more than he had ever dared hope for. Orla sat and suggested he do the same. He sat formally across from her.

"I'm honored to be given a position in your household, Your Highness. How may I be of service?" Ciarán asked cautiously.

Orla snorted and Ciarán looked at her in confusion.

"Please, of course you are welcome, Ciarán. You have no idea who Olav has tried already. Ponces, all of them. And you can call me Orla." She laughed at the thought of Ciarán's predecessors.

"Your Highness, with respect, I have been given a position of trust in your household and I feel that I should maintain decorum in that position." He straightened even further.

Orla stared at him for a moment and her smile faltered. "Very well, Captain. Have you been well?"

Ciarán nodded. "I have. My brother has helped me adjust to my new circumstances."

Orla looked at the neatly pinned sleeve, bereft of his forearm and hand. He tried his best not to fidget. Scrutiny of any kind, in regards to his arm, always set him on edge, but Orla deserved to see what he would otherwise hide. She was concerned about his formal attitude but she was sure she could thaw his frozen exterior in no time and then she would have her old friend back.

"Captain Allyn, you will be an asset and welcome company for me. We will not discuss any shortcomings as I am sure you are more than qualified for the responsibilities you have been given. Do you understand my meaning?" she said.

"Aye, Your Highness," he nodded.

"Good. You have had a long day after a long journey. Thank you for meeting with me" she said kindly and stood.

Ciarán rose and bowed, making his way to the door. He was stopped once more by Orla.

"Ciarán?" she said timidly.

He stared at the door, waiting for her to speak.

"I'm so glad you are here. I missed you."

It was barely a whisper but he nodded his head to acknowledge that he heard her and left the room. In the hallway, he leaned against the wall and let out a breath. He wanted to vomit or pass out or possibly both. He didn't know if he would be able to stand this torture. He thought he had gotten over her but seeing her again just made his heart long for her even more. He sighed and went off to see if he could find his rooms in the maze of the castle hallways.

Adjusting to life in Fadersogn took longer than Ciarán thought it should. The castle was drafty and cold, the weather in Fadersogn was not as temperate as the weather in Eiremor. It was also much larger than Phelan and Meara's castle and he found himself lost on numerous occasions. Furthermore, Orla did not stray far from the castle on most days and did not really need protection. She tried her best to include him in her routine but it was clear that a guard was not needed on a daily basis. He'd begun to get bored when the opportunity for a trip outside the castle walls presented itself.

Orla and Ciarán were returning from the countryside after attending the christening of the first-born child of one of Olav's cousins. Olav had wanted to attend but a last-minute communication from Noregfjord meant he needed to stay behind and attend a council meeting. They had been gone for four days and Ciarán had enjoyed every minute of it. He and Orla spent the days of riding, which Orla preferred over carriages, talking and laughing. It almost felt as if the war had never happened.

They were rounding a bend in the road when Orla's horse spooked and threw her to the ground. Ciarán pulled up short, dropping to the ground and quickly grabbing the reins of her horse, calming it before it could trample her. He knelt beside her to check for injuries.

"Orla, are you alright?" he asked with concern.

Orla nodded and then looked up from checking her ankle. Her eyes widened as she looked past him. At that moment, Ciarán felt a sword tip in his back. He chided himself silently and raised his arms in the air.

"We don't want any trouble," he said to the person wielding the sword.

"Well you found it anyway, m'lord," the bandit said.

"These are some fine horses," a second bandit chimed in, grabbing the reins Ciarán had dropped.

"They aren't yours," Ciarán said through gritted teeth.

The bandits laughed.

"They are now. What else have you got?" the sword-wielding bandit asked. "Check the woman."

Ciarán bristled as Orla stood quickly and then winced in pain. The second bandit walked into his line of vision and he saw that the man had covered his head with a sack with crude holes in it. The man started to reach for Orla and Ciarán sprung into action, drawing his sword in one smooth motion as he kicked the man to the ground. He turned on the man who had first held him captive with fury.

"You won't touch her!" he shouted.

The bandit parried a blow aimed at his head. Ciarán and the bandit began fighting in earnest. The bandit was a decent swordsman but was hindered because he too had a sack over his head. Ciarán was getting the upper hand when he heard Orla yelp. He turned to check on her and the bandit he was fighting took the opportunity to grab the horses and mount one. Orla was struggling in the other bandit's arms and Ciarán assessed the situation quickly. He was about to attack the man when the one on the horses yelled out.

"Leave her! Come on!"

The bandit holding Orla shoved her towards Ciarán, pushing him off balance for a moment as he caught her. The bandit jumped on the second horse and they both rode away.

"Bloody hell!" Ciarán raged. He looked back at Orla, who seemed shaken but no worse. "Did he hurt you?"

Orla shook her head. "No, but I think I hurt my ankle in the fall from my horse."

Ciarán nodded. He looked around and saw a stump near the edge of the road. He helped her to sit.

"I need to check if it is broken," Ciarán said.

Orla extended her leg and Ciarán let it rest on his knee as he removed her shoe. He lightly felt along the bones of her ankle and moved it from side to side. Orla hissed at the pain the motion caused.

"I'm sorry. The good news is I don't believe it's broken, only sprained."

Orla sighed. "What do we do now?"

Ciarán stood and got his bearings.

"I remember where we are. There is a small town about an hour's walk from here. Do you think, if I helped you, you could walk that far?" Ciarán hated to suggest it but he would not leave her alone, lest the bandits come back and do much worse than stealing horses.

Orla nodded. Ciarán searched the forest around them and found a suitable walking stick. He helped Orla to stand and let her rest some of her weight on his arm as they headed towards the town.

After twenty minutes of walking, making much slower progress than Ciarán had hoped, a giant thunderclap made both Orla and Ciarán jump. Ciarán looked up at the sky and cursed again. He tried to hurry Orla along, taking on more of her weight, but he did not think they would make it to the town before the storm hit. They passed the forest and were on the edge of a clearing. Ciarán could see a farm barn in the distance. Perhaps they could make it to the safety of the barn.

Orla and Ciarán got halfway to the barn when the first drops of rain started. Ciarán weighed his options as quickly as possible.

"Orla, do you think you could hold onto my neck tightly?" Ciarán asked.

"What are you thinking?"

"I will carry you the rest of the way but you will have to hold on tight," he said,

Orla shook her head. "How? It can't be easy for you."

Ciarán closed his eyes for a moment, determined not to let himself get angry at his perceived deficiencies. He knew she did not mean it that way but was still getting used to believing it himself. He opened his eyes and did his best to give her a reassuring smile.

"Trust me?" he asked.

Orla nodded and put her arms around his neck. Ciarán adjusted her position, then reached down and swooped her up. The rain began pounding harder and Ciarán did his best to run towards the barn. It felt like an eternity but they finally made it inside. It was empty and Ciarán could not tell if it was abandoned or merely unoccupied at the moment. He set Orla down gently. She was soaked and shivering. They both were.

"Let me see if I can find a horse blanket or something. Sit here and rest," Ciarán said as he helped her to a bale of hay.

Ciarán searched the barn and found some tackle in the back. There was a horse blanket and several saddles. It was good news to him, it meant that when the rain stopped, there might be a chance of a farm house close by. He brought the blanket back and wrapped it around Orla, then sat next to her. She continued to shiver and he did the only thing he could think of to help make her warmer, he wrapped his arm around her.

Orla's teeth chattered. "Thh... ank... you."

Ciarán smiled and rubbed his arm up and down, hoping to give her more heat from the friction.

"It's my job," he said.

Orla started to warm up and she turned towards him with sincerity in her eyes.

"No, I mean thank you for everything. For coming here in the first place. I missed you," she said.

Ciarán scratched behind his ear and started to turn away. Orla put her hand on his cheek. She stared into his face, waiting for him to meet her eyes. When he did, she smiled softly. His breath caught in his throat. The rain had made the perfume in her hair soap stronger. He inhaled the scent. He hadn't had time to think about how close she was during their walk or when he was carrying her, but now it was just her and he was thrown adrift.

"Orla..." Ciarán couldn't find the words.

She leaned in and kissed him. Ciarán wanted to pull away but he was powerless to do so. He deepened the kiss and she responded, wrapping her arms around him. Ciarán held her closer, lost in the feeling of her against him. He couldn't get enough of her, tangling his hand in her hair. Orla's hand reached down to loosen the strings of his shirt and he froze. Orla continued peppering his face and neck with kisses and Ciarán stilled her hand with his own.

"Orla, stop," Ciarán pleaded.

"I don't want to stop," she said.

"But you must, please."

Orla leaned back and looked into his eyes., love and anguish warring in them. She bit her lip, fighting herself.

"I'm sorry," she said, realizing her mistake.

"It's my fault," Ciarán replied.

"No... I should—" Orla started to explain but was cut off.

Ciarán stood. "The rain's stopped. I'm going to see if there is a farmer nearby. They have horses, perhaps we can get a message to the castle."

Orla nodded but Ciarán did not wait for an answer. He needed to get some air and calm his emotions.

Ciarán was able to send word to the castle about the ambush. The farmer was happy to host Her Royal Highness and her guard until help arrived. The farmer's wife bandaged Orla's sprained ankle and fed both she and Ciarán a lovely stew. They were excellent hosts and Orla made a mental note to have them rewarded for their kindness.

Olav and his guards pulled up outside and Ciarán went out to welcome them. He relayed all that had happened to Olav, along with a description of the bandits. Olav promised to find them and sent two of his guards to investigate the area. Olav thanked Ciarán and went into the farmhouse.

Ciarán watched their reunion from the doorway, Olav the concerned husband and Orla the reassuring wife. He found himself becoming incredibly jealous. He had seen them together before but, in this instance, he would have preferred to be the one comforting Orla. It pained him further when Olav easily swept Orla into his arms and carried her outside, seating her on his horse. Ciarán nodded at Olav and mounted his own horse, riding behind his future King and Queen. His heart ached. This was indeed torture but he was helpless to avoid it.

CHAPTER ELEVEN

Over time, the effects of the tonic slowly wore off; each day he coughed more and more. Once again, Ciarán began coughing blood and feeling exhausted and generally unwell. At dinner one evening, the coughing became so bad that he had to excuse himself from the table and stayed in his rooms the rest of the night dealing with the pain in his chest and spitting out blood into the washbasin. Orla had fled the table with barely contained tears. Quinn had sullenly fed the meat from his plate to the cat at his feet while Erik and Runa whispered quietly to each other and Olav chased after his wife.

"Orla?" Olav caught up with her.

Orla turned, swiping angrily at her cheeks. Olav cupped her face in his hands.

"We must talk about this situation. You can't keep it bottled inside," he said.

Orla bit her lip. "He's not getting any better. We are losing him and... and I'm powerless. He's going to die, just like his mother, isn't he?"

Olav nodded. "Aye, I'm afraid so. The symptoms and progression of the illness are the same as what she suffered."

Orla trembled. "Why didn't I see it? We were shielded from the worst of it but I should have recognized the similarities. Does he know?"

"Sometimes love can blind us to reality. He has known for some time now and has accepted his fate."

It was too much for Orla and she collapsed into Olav, sobs wracking her body. He helped her to their rooms and sat with her while she let herself finally admit that Ciarán would not survive his illness. Olav didn't know which was worse, losing someone you loved quickly, as he had lost Lochlann, or watching your love deteriorate via a crippling illness.

Orla had once again confined him to his rooms and he was forced to see a new physician almost every day. Each had their own cure, most of which smelled awful and tasted even worse. One of the physicians, not the original ponce who had wanted to bleed him dry, but an equally annoying one, had demanded that he now remain on bed rest and that visitors be severely limited. This particular physician firmly believed in *bad airs* and was not dissuaded from those beliefs when Ciarán explained all about the disease that was killing him. He had recommended the Queen and her family stay away, in case the disease was contagious, and Orla had scoffed and sent the man packing. When Orla informed Ciarán she would have to find a new physician, and the reasoning behind it, he had quietly convinced her that no more were needed. She reluctantly agreed but also persuaded him to stay on bed rest and limit visitors. It was a compromise that eased both of their minds.

Daily visits from Erik and Runa helped to lift his spirits a great deal, but his coughing fits had become so violent and so frequent that he was loathe to allow them to see him in such a state. Small spatters of blood came up when he coughed and he did his best to hide it from Orla, going so far as to burn the bloodstained handkerchiefs in the fireplace of his sitting room. Olav quietly re-supplied them when he overheard a servant ask where he might purchase them in bulk as Master Ciarán's kept disappearing.

He was lying in bed reading and dozing, when suddenly Quinn appeared at his side. He jumped a little in surprise, but tried to seem unaffected, hiding it behind a cough.

"Hello Uncle," Quinn said brightly.

"Bloody hell, you aren't supposed to be here," Ciarán said gruffly.

Quinn shrugged. "I know. But I hardly think it is fair Erik and Runa were allowed to see you, and then when I was finally ready, Mother suggested I wait until you were feeling better."

Ciarán sat up straighter and gave Quinn a questioning look. "Quinn, did you freeze everyone again?"

Quinn shook his head sheepishly. "Not this time. I told them I wanted to read in the library and then, when the coast was clear, I came here. They don't pay me much attention anyway."

Ciarán laughed. "You are such a tenacious lad. They pay more attention than you believe."

"I needed to talk to you," Quinn said seriously. "I have been trying to think about how to talk to you and I just don't know what to say. I'm sorry I have been avoiding you."

Quinn twisted his hands, averting his eyes, but peeked sidelong at Ciarán. Ciarán nodded in forgiveness and patted the spot next to him on the bed. Quinn climbed onto the bed and sat cross-legged, picking up the book Ciarán had discarded. He studied the spine, and after a moment, he spoke.

"You have never treated me like a child. Erik and Runa are always whispering to each other and keeping things from me, but you would tell me the truth, right?" he asked.

Ciarán nodded. "I will always answer you in the best

way I can, with as much honesty as I possess."

"Are you going to die soon?" Quinn blurted.

Ciarán shrugged. "I cannot say when I will die. No man can tell the future."

"But you will die sooner rather than later?" the young boy asked.

"Aye, unfortunately, my time is near."

Quinn nodded. He thought for a long moment and Ciarán studied his godson. The boy was very precocious but also very intelligent. His blue eyes missed nothing. He was often intense and quiet but then would stun Ciarán with some profound knowledge or idea. He had a very distinct memory as well, as if he could take a picture of a moment and define every second in detail. It was a joy for Ciarán to discuss all manner of topics with Quinn. He was able to talk to the boy as if he were a small adult rather than a young boy, barely a teenager.

"I'm different," he blurted as he stared at Ciarán, watching for his reaction.

"Aye, you are unique and you have magic," Ciarán observed.

"Yes, but no one else does," he said quietly and broke the eye contact.

"Your mother has magic, you get it from her."

Quinn nodded. "So does uncle Kellan. They are the products of true love and everyone knows that is how magic is born. But Erik and Runa don't have magic, so if Mother and Papa were true love, wouldn't all of us have magic? And I don't look like them either."

Ciarán thought a moment. "Perhaps it skips around in the second generation? Your mother, uncle, and their tutor are the only people I have known with magic before you came along. So I do not know the rules of how it is passed on to a child. Perhaps not all children of true love are magical."

Quinn narrowed his eyes at Ciarán, searching for something and not finding it.

"I don't think it works that way," he said with finality.

"Spit it out, lad. What are you asking?" Ciarán asked after an uncomfortable moment.

Quinn twisted his hands in his lap and his eyebrows knitted in concentration, then shot up. Ciarán could see he'd made a decision.

"Well, I have magic and I don't look like Mother and Papa. Erik looks like Papa and Runa looks like them both. I don't think I look like any of my family. I love Papa and I don't want to hurt him but I don't think he is my father. Do you?" Quinn asked seriously.

Ciarán was silent. He did not know what to tell the boy and he did not feel like this was a conversation that he should be having with him. Olav loved all three of his children equally. He made sure that each child was treated uniquely and given room to grow into the well-rounded, capable adults he knew they could be. Each of his children would be good citizens and assets to their kingdom and its people. It pained Ciarán to think Quinn did not feel equal to Erik or Runa in Olav's eyes.

"Quinn, you are a very astute boy. It was a proud day when your parents made me your godfather. I could think of no greater honor than to be responsible for your education. I cannot honestly tell you why you have magic and the others do not. It would not be my place if I did know. Your mother is a faithful and honorable woman, do not doubt her devotion to your father. What I can tell you is that you are a very special boy and that you will make your parents proud," he replied.

Quinn stared into space for a moment. "Do you love mother?"

Ciarán choked, setting off another a coughing fit. Ciarán turned away for a glass of water, hiding his shock at the blunt question. Once the coughing subsided, and he could delay no longer, he answered, "I love all of you."

"But do you love Mother the most?" Quinn prodded.

Ciarán sighed and tried to change the subject. "You are

my favorite godson. Don't tell Erik and Runa I said that."

Quinn laughed. "You aren't their godfather."

"No, I'm all yours." Ciarán smiled and ruffled his hair.

Quinn protested and then jabbed Ciarán in the side. They fake wrestled for a moment and then Quinn got serious again. "You didn't answer the question," he pointed out.

"You noticed," Ciarán said. Quinn nodded. Ciarán thought for a moment. He knew that he would not be able to lie to Quinn. The child would only hound him until he was forced to give him the truth. "Quinn, when you find a person that makes you happy, promise me that you will tell them how you feel. You won't wait or let misunderstandings get in the way. You will proudly declare your love and not let circumstances get in the way. Love is the most important emotion of all and if you love someone, you are more than worthy of them," he said honestly.

Quinn nodded. "I promise, cross my heart."

"Your mother will live in my heart for eternity. It belongs to her and her alone. I will love her until my last breath and beyond because death itself is not strong enough to quash it," Ciarán said as he tried to swallow the lump in his throat and found that it was too difficult. He looked at Quinn expectantly, silently asking him if he understood. Quinn nodded and they sat in amiable silence, each lost in their own thoughts.

At last Quinn said, "Uncle Ciarán?"

"Hmm?"

"I would have been proud to call you my father," he said.

Ciarán wrapped the boy in a hug and rested his cheek upon the top of his head.

"I would have been honored to have you as my son," he replied.

Outside the bedroom door, Orla covered her mouth with her hand and fled out of the rooms and down the corridor as fast and as quietly as she could.

AMBER RAINEY

Orla was in the nursery with Erik and Runa when the message came. They had been having a delightful tea party complete with imaginary guests. Orla was the magical queen of the fairies, while Erik was a gallant knight who had saved the kingdom from an evil dragon. Runa was, of course, the misunderstood dragon, who had been locked in the dungeons and unfairly charged with disorderly conduct. Erik was arguing that dragons shouldn't be rescued. The room was full of laughter and joy and the pageboy who had come to summon her to the throne room was wary of interrupting.

The boy had been there when the message arrived and his normally jovial king's attitude changed almost immediately, barking orders and sending him to fetch Her Majesty immediately. He relayed the message that King Olav required her presence and she left her children in the care of their nurse while she wiped off the glitter that had served as her fairy dust.

On the way to the throne room, she met up with Ciarán, who had also been summoned, and he offered to escort her the rest of the way. Orla took his offered arm and they walked in a companionable silence, each lost in wondering why their normal routines had been interrupted. Upon entering the throne room, Ciarán bowed to Orla and then to her husband. He waited while Orla took her seat on her throne and then looked at King Olav expectantly. The King was visibly distressed and Ciarán frowned.

Olav looked from the letter in his hands, first to Ciarán and then to Orla. Studying each of them and weighing his options. He wiped a hand over his face and cleared his throat. He did not know how he was going to break this news to them. His own heart was full of sorrow.

"Olav? What is it?" Orla asked with growing trepidation. She laid a comforting hand on his arm. He squeezed her hand in gratitude.

"My darling, it is with extremely great difficulty that I must tell you that your father is very ill. It is believed he will not recover and your mother has asked that you return to say goodbye before he is gone," Olav said gently.

Orla gasped and her hand flew to her mouth. She shared a look of horror with Ciarán, then she turned back to her husband. "I will make arrangements to go immediately. If I ride instead of take the carriage, it will be faster. You and the children can follow after, if you wish." She paced back and forth as she spoke.

Ciarán spoke up. "By your leave, Your Majesty, I will go and make arrangements for you."

"Wait, Captain Allyn." Olav stopped him. "I agree that Her Majesty should return to Eiremor as soon as possible, and that you should accompany her on this journey. However, there is further news I must share with you before you depart."

Ciarán gave a short bow and waited. He was anxious to start the journey and give Orla time to see her father before he passed.

Olav hesitated and Orla squeezed his arm again to give him the strength to continue. He smiled gratefully then looked at Ciarán with sympathy. Ciarán's heart was in his throat. What could be worse than the death of Orla's father?

"Ciarán, it is with regret that I must inform you Captain Lochlann Allyn has..." Tears ran down Olav's cheeks and he struggled to finish his sentence. "...died while serving in his duties to King Phelan. May the Gods grant him favor in paradise."

Ciarán's knees buckled and, without thinking, Orla rushed to his side. Olav also stood and came to his side, laying a hand on his shoulder.

Ciarán shivered and whispered, "No, it cannot be true."

AMBER RAINEY

"I am sorry for your loss," Olav said and left the two of them alone in the throne room so that he may mourn the passing of his dearest friend in private.

Orla watched him go and was torn between the two men. Her heart ached for both of them. Ciarán lost the last family he'd ever known and Olav the love of his life. She struggled to do the right thing in this moment but Ciarán looked so defeated that, in the end, she stayed with him until he recovered enough to prepare for the journey back to Eiremor.

Orla and Ciarán journeyed back to Eiremor with a small retinue of only four guards. Orla felt that if the six of them rode hard, then they could make it back faster and she was correct. They made the journey in only two days as opposed to the four it would normally take. They were exhausted, having barely stopped for food and a change of horses, and arrived just as the sun was setting on the second day. They were immediately shown to their rooms and given dinner. After a brief rest, they were led to the sitting room of King Phelan's suite where Meara awaited them.

Meara related the story of what happened to them as best she could. Phelan and Lochlann had been returning from a visit to the shipbuilder, who had been commissioned with a new design, when they were attacked by thieves on the road. The guards, Lochlann and Phelan had fought them off valiantly and eventually got what they believed was the upper hand. Two of the guards had been lost but the other two returned with Phelan and Lochlann. The two surviving men had injuries, but nothing that appeared to warrant any concerns—minor scratches. Lochlann made it all the way back to the castle before collapsing in the courtyard as he dismounted his horse. It was then discovered that he had been hiding a stab wound in his shoulder from a weapon laced with poison. Upon this realization, Phelan was immediately examined and a scratch on his arm was found to have also been laced with poison. This poison had no known cure.

Lochlann, having been exposed to a greater dose of the poison in his wound, died that night and that was when the messenger had been dispatched to Orla. The physicians gave a sour outlook on the prognosis of Phelan recovering, but as of now, he was still with them, thank the Gods. Perhaps he could fight it and live. There would, of course, be a funeral with full military honors for Captain Allyn, but they had waited to proceed until Orla and Ciarán could return.

Meara was distraught and unable to carry on. Orla comforted her mother and watched Ciarán struggle with the news of how his brother had died. She longed to help him but her mother was her first priority. One of Meara's trusted advisors, quietly took Ciarán aside and asked if he would like to see his brother. He nodded and was led away. Kellan met him in the hall and they shared a silent greeting before Ciarán continued to follow the advisor.

Ciarán laid a shaking hand on his brother's shroud. Ciarán lifted back the shroud to stare at his brother's face, wanting to see it without the cloth in the way. Lochlann's military medals had been pinned to his chest and someone had thought to pick some of the flowers from the meadow for him to hold. The last of his family lay there on a slab, unmoving and cold. The man he had always put on a pedestal, brought low by poison. He had never thought he would outlive his brother and now the stark realization that he had was more than he could bear. He collapsed in a heap next to Lochlann and sobbed.

Olav, Erik, and Runa arrived a day later. The children were very young and put into the care of the nursery while the adults kept watch over Phelan. Ciarán had stood vigil at Lochlann's side until Olav entered the chapel. He looked up at Olav, barely recognizing him through the grief. Olav spoke quietly.

"Ciarán, Orla has asked me to fetch you. She says you must eat if you can."

Ciarán nodded but stared at the shrouded remains in front of him. The men sat in silence until Ciarán noticed Olav concealing a sob. Ciarán stood and laid a hand on his brother's hand. He looked back at Olav and straightened, composing himself as best he could. Their eyes met and a silent understanding passed between them.

"I will keep watch with him until you return," Olav said.

Ciarán nodded and left the chapel. Shaking, Olav stood and went to Lochlann's side. He pulled back the shroud and stared at Lochlann's face. Even in death, the man still looked brave. Olav let his tears flow freely as he bent down and kissed Lochlann's cheek.

The next morning, Captain Lochlann Allyn was laid on a barge and set to sea. Orla offered to do the honors of setting the barge aflame and Ciarán accepted gratefully. The magical fire would burn better than one started by arrows. The ceremony was a quiet affair but well-attended as Lochlann was beloved by his men. The other officers took it upon themselves to offer their condolences to Ciarán and he stood stoically throughout the ordeal.

Afterwards, Queen Meara led him to a small room where Lochlann's things had been taken. She presented to Ciarán the sextant she and King Phelan had gifted Lochlann years ago upon his attaining the rank of Captain and told him that it was Lochlann's last wish that it should be passed onto him. Ciarán nodded his thanks and Queen Meara gave him a brief hug, quickly returning to her husband's side.

Once she had taken her leave, Ciarán crumpled to the floor sobbing, Orla holding him close, fighting her own tears. He'd thought there were no more tears left, but it seemed they would never stop. Orla spoke softly to him, lauding Lochlann, and trying to make Ciarán understand he was not alone, but in the end, she sobbed along with him. Lochlann had always treated her like a sister and she would miss his good-natured teasing.

Later that day, Orla was summoned to her father's chambers and she went only to find it was his last hours. She and her mother stayed with him until the end and it pained her to see how heartbroken her mother was when faced with the reality that Phelan would not pull through. Orla let her tears flow freely and kissed her father's forehead one last time. She sat with her mother throughout the night, who refused to leave her husband's side. She did not want anyone to touch him.

Eventually, Orla and the maids were able to convince Queen Meara that they needed to see to Phelan's body before it became unsightly and smelled. She would not want to remember him that way. Orla helped her mother to bathe and then sat next to her in the bed, humming and stroking her hair until Meara fell asleep. It was something her mother did to comfort her as a child and she was happy to return the favor.

Two days after he died, the King was given a proper funeral complete with pomp and circumstance. The line of people who wished to pay their respects stretched for miles. The Queen was helped throughout the ceremony by her children. Meara seemed to shrink in on herself, her skin paler than it had ever been and her lips taking on a bluish tint, as if her heart could no longer function without Phelan's. She leaned heavily on Kellan, now King of Eiremor. She lovingly kissed her husband one last time and then ordered the funeral pyre be lit. Orla and Kellan combined their magic to make the fire more brilliant. It could be seen for miles around the castle in all directions.

Many would say that Queen Meara died with her husband as she never regained the light she once had. When she died a year later—likely of a broken heart—few were surprised.

AMBER RAINEY

Orla lay staring at the ceiling the night of her father's funeral. She had cried so much, she had no more tears. It had been a very long time since she had allowed herself so much sorrow. She ached for her lost father and her mother who was left behind without the man she loved. Orla knew her parents had a special bond most people never experienced and she knew her father and mother always completed each other. They had promised they would be with each other forever, no matter the hardships thrown their way, and never let go of that promise, even in the darkest of times. It made Orla think of another promise: *I will come back.*

Ciarán had come back time and again for her. Even after he left for war and she was convinced he was gone forever, when she had let him down by not believing in him, he had still come back for her. Lochlann had told her that when he asked Ciarán how he'd lived through all his suffering, how he had stayed sane, Ciarán replied that he simply thought of home and of her. He promised her he would return and he was a man of his word.

Orla had shed so many tears the night of his return. Tears of guilt and remorse for letting even one second of doubt into her mind. She'd thought they would be parted forever after she left Eiremor, but then he came back to her yet again. It wasn't in a way she'd ever imagined but she was glad for it all the same.

She had overheard a conversation between Ciarán and Lochlann the day the latter left for the eastern borders of Fadersogn. Ciarán told his brother he was rethinking his position as Orla's guard. Lochlann looked at his brother and smiled sadly.

He said, "Your heart belongs near hers even if they cannot be together as you would wish."

Ciarán started to protest but Lochlann interrupted.

"You may wish to deny it, brother, but you and she will always be linked. You are too stubborn to admit it but I can see there will never be another for you."

Orla had run off, unable to listen to the rest of the conversation. It had been rude of her to eavesdrop, but in reality, she couldn't hear any more. She had not understood the depth of Ciarán's continued devotion to her, even after all the mistakes she had made. She'd let him down and yet he still remained faithful. She did not deserve his loyalty.

The first years of their new relationship had been awkward but eventually they settled into a rhythm. Olav gladly welcomed Ciarán's wisdom, especially in naval matters and dealings with pirates. Ciarán hated them, with good reason, and wished to put an end to piracy once and for all. When Olav became king, he'd gifted Ciarán with a ship and, with Olav's permission, it was christened *The Return*. The King trusted Ciarán and saw that he was a valuable ally in keeping the kingdom safe. Ciarán had been very observant during his time as a slave to the pirates and possessed invaluable knowledge about their movements and tactics. The admirals of the kingdom frequently consulted him and, more than once, Ciarán's information resulted in the successful capture of a pirate ship.

Orla thought about how much Ciarán must have given up to be in service to her and Olav. Sure, he treated her children as if he was the loving Uncle they called him but he had no children of his own, no female companionship and not even a home of his own. He had quarters aboard *The Return* but only used them when he was away on diplomatic missions. Most times he let the captain of the ship run it with his guidance. When he was not away, he had rooms in the castle and he served as a personal guard to her and the children. She could not recall him having any type of personal life outside his royal duties.

Orla cringed inwardly at her own selfishness. She had

been so consumed with the death of her father that she did not realize how much Ciarán must be suffering with the death of the last remaining member of his family. She still had her brother and her mother but he had no one. She had allowed him to be alone since the funeral without offering him someone to talk to or any solace at his loss. He had continued his duties as her guard with no complaint at all, helping her with the planning and carrying out every errand she asked of him. She intended to rectify that situation and she resolved to do it this instant.

She turned over in her bed, noticing Olav staring out the window. He had been mostly silent since arriving and had not been sleeping well. She knew that Lochlann had been dear to Olav and he was dealing with the grief as best he could.

"Olav?" she asked tentatively.

He turned to face her.

"I need to talk to Ciarán," she said timidly. She did not know how to convey what she wanted.

Olav nodded.

Orla started to get out of the bed but felt she owed him an explanation. "It's just... he and I... he has been my best friend and he lost everything and I..."

Olav crossed the room and grasped Orla's hand in his own. "Orla, I understand. You love Ciarán and he needs you. He needs to know that you love him right now."

Orla's eyes widened. "What are you saying?"

"I'm saying go be with him tonight. You can console him more than you can me at this moment," Olav said sadly.

"Olav, if you are not well I can stay with you. I know Lochlann meant a great deal to you." Orla looked at him with sympathy shining in her eyes.

Olav nodded. "He was... I cannot... He was everything. Suffice it to say, I wish for you to tell Ciarán how you feel. Our lives are too short to suppress our feelings. I know you care for me and our children, but Ciarán does not know he still has people who love him. Lochlann would want him to know he is not alone."

Orla nodded and Olav went back to the window, slumping down in a chair. He watched the moon reflecting off the waters in the bay and stared at the ships bobbing in the water. He waited for Orla to leave the room so he could cry, yet again, at Lochlann's death.

Orla threw on a dressing gown and walked out of her room to the room across the hall. She could tell he was still awake as she could see the candlelight coming from beneath the door. Orla knocked, then opened the door. Ciarán must not have heard her, for he was standing in stony silence staring at the firelight, his head resting against his arm on the mantle. Orla's breath caught in her throat upon realizing that he was shirtless. She followed the lines of scars all across his back and arms and she felt new tears forming in her eyes at all that he must have suffered as a slave. Her sob caught Ciarán's attention and he straightened.

"Your Highness? Is everything okay?" Ciarán asked with concern.

"No, Ciarán, it is not," she returned, tears still flowing down her cheeks.

Ciarán was loathe to see her so upset. She had been very close to her father and this was the first time she had lost someone so dear. He walked over to her and fought the urge to wipe the tears from her cheeks, as he had done when they were young. He searched her eyes for something to give him a clue of what she needed.

"I am sorry for the loss of your dear father, you must be so distraught. Is there anything I can do to make it more bearable?" he asked.

"Thank you, I am very saddened at the death of my father, but that is not why I am here," Orla said.

She could not help but look down at his chest, the lean muscles covered in dark hair that trailed down beneath his pants. She noticed more scars, only half hidden by the hair and wished she could remove the proof of all that had been done to him. This part of him had always been hidden from her. She knew, intrinsically, what tortures he had been subjected to for Lochlann had informed her in detail when she demanded it. She had just never seen it with her own eyes.

Ciarán noticed where her eyes had wandered. He scratched behind his ear, blushing. He had never let Orla see the extent of the torture he had received as a slave to the pirates. He was embarrassed by the scars and disfigurement of his arm.

"I apologize, Your Highness, let me become more decent and I will endeavor to help you as best I can," he said.

Orla laid a hand on his bicep to stop him from retreating and shook her head. "Ciarán, you have been a most loyal and trusted friend even when I betrayed you. I don't deserve your devotion."

"You deserve the world, Orla. I believe it is *you* who does not deserve a personal guard with a handicap such as mine, yet you still keep me in your employ." Ciarán gave a self-deprecating laugh.

Orla put her hands on his cheeks, forcing him to look in her eyes. "I would give you much more, if it were in my power. I would have you happy with a home and a family of your own. Not beholden to me, or my family, out of your sense of duty for what I might want."

They were so close, she did not miss the look that crossed his features. He stared at her with unabashed love and devotion.

"Orla, it has never been a burden for me to serve you. You must know where my heart lies." He spoke softly, afraid of breaking the spell.

"I have been so selfish the past years. No, all my life, when it comes to you. I have taken you for granted. I have tried not to think of the sacrifices you have made for me—I couldn't let them affect me. I have let you mourn the death of your brother alone, and he died trying to save my father. Your family has given so much in service to mine, and I would wish to rectify the situation. You must know, Ciarán, that I would release you from your vows of service if you wished it. I do know that you love my children as if they were your blood, and you are loyal to my husband, but I am positive that Olav would not be averse to setting you up comfortably, or even allowing you to choose your home wherever you wish it to be."

Orla was terrified Ciarán would, indeed, wish to be something other than her personal guard, but she felt honor-bound to release him if that was his wish. It was time she thought of his happiness.

Ciarán allowed himself to rest his forehead against hers. "Orla, my home will always be with you. I know you belong to another but I must tell you that my soul aches when we are apart. A piece of me dies inside every time I must leave on a mission and is reborn the minute I see you again. I could never leave you, even if you demanded it of me."

"Ciarán," Orla choked out, then kissed him.

She had resisted him for so long, and she had sworn that she would be faithful to her husband, but in this instance, her heart was yelling so loud for the man in front of her, that she did the only thing that would alleviate the pain. Ciarán stiffened for only a moment before his arm was around her. They kissed until neither of them could deny a breath for any longer.

Orla clung to Ciarán and he buried his nose in her neck, attempting to regain some semblance of calm. Orla thought for a moment and then she left his arms.

Ciarán's shoulders slumped as he realized the mistake he had made. "Forgive me, I forgot myself, I..." he trailed off as Orla shut the door and locked it.

She removed her dressing gown and he swallowed the lump in his throat. This was going too far, he must remember his place.

"Orla, we can't. I am not your husband and he is across the hall," he said.

Orla shrugged. "Ciarán, I need to be with you. Please?"

"It's not right. It will ruin you." Ciarán groaned as Orla returned to him, lightly stroking her hands over his chest.

"Shh," she said, as she put her fingers on his lips. "Just this once, please Ciarán. I cannot stay away from you any longer."

He groaned, unable to deny her anything. He had always been hers to command.

"Aye," he said and kissed her as if she was the only thing tethering him to this world.

Ciarán made love to Orla, and was so wrapped up in her, he did not notice the candles flickering to life around his room. They stayed with each other throughout the night, talking until they fell asleep. She left early in the morning to return to her rooms, but not before watching him sleep for a few precious moments. This man, whom she loved above all others, was the most handsome and forgiving man she had ever known. She let a silent tear fall for all that they might never experience together. She was so tired of crying. She had made her own future and now she must accept it.

Later that day, Orla sought Ciarán out, for she had not seen him since the previous evening. She had once again been busy helping her mother, and Ciarán had been helping her brother with preparations for his investiture. She found him sitting in the meadow, twirling forget-me-nots in his fingers, lost in thought. Orla sat next to him and for a while they did not speak. She studied his profile and he finally looked at her.

"I thought I would find you here," she said with a smile.

He nodded. "Aye, this place holds many happy memories. I brought some of Lochlann's things and buried them by the tree."

Ciarán gestured towards the willow tree.

"He would have wanted me to keep them but I wanted

something here in our spot, so that I could visit and remember," he said.

"That is a brilliant idea. I remember a time when the three of us were carefree with the whole world ahead of us. I never imagined our life like this," Orla said wistfully.

Ciarán looked away, still twirling the flower in his hand. He bit his lip for a moment and then looked back at her.

"I apologize for my lapse in judgement. I was emotional and lost. It can never happen again, Orla. It would put you in danger and I would not forgive myself if any harm came to you." Ciarán looked at her with remorse and guilt.

Orla huffed, "Do not apologize to me. I agree that it can never happen again, I owe it to Olav to be faithful to my vows, but it was the happiest night of my life."

Ciarán looked astonished. "You mean that?"

"I do. It was everything I hoped for and more. Ciarán, if I could go back in time and change everything I would." Orla said sadly.

"I know, love," Ciarán said.

"Do you remember when I was studying prophecy magic?" she asked.

Ciarán nodded. She had been good at it but he knew she had seen something she did not like and decided against developing that part of her magic. She wanted to be master of her own fate.

"I saw some of our future. It did not make me happy. I saw you being sworn into my service. It was fuzzy but I refused to believe it. My husband would not be a servant. I did not like what I had seen, but perhaps if I had finished the vision, I could have changed it. I could have waited for you instead of getting married.

"Orla, we can wish to change the past but it is as fruitful as trying to stop the waves in the ocean. Some things are out of our control. I do not fault you for wishing your future to remain unknown, it might only have caused you undue grief." He lifted the forget-me-nots and put the stem behind her ear. "Still the loveliest maid in the meadow."

Orla laughed and rested her head against his shoulder. "And you still my noble servant?" she asked.

"Forever," he said.

Orla and Ciarán stared out across the meadow, both dreaming of a different life and yet coming to terms with the one they had been given.

Ciarán heard the bells ringing and smiled, breathing a sigh of relief. The bells meant that the new prince or princess had finally arrived. Luckily, the pregnancy had been easy on Orla, it seemed to lift her spirits after the death of her father. These past few weeks, he had been remanded to more duties involving the children since the physicians demanded that Orla must rest. He did not envy their task; she nearly knocked one of them unconscious when she threw a book at his head for suggesting she was possibly getting too round to be playing on the floor with Runa.

Ciarán looked back at Erik, who had been riding on his back. Erik's eyes were wide; he had been too young to remember Runa's birth, but now at six, he had definitely been interested in waiting for the child to be born. He asked nearly every day if the baby had come yet and whined that it was taking too long. Patience was not a virtue he possessed yet.

"It seems your sibling has made its appearance," Ciarán said jovially.

"Aye, I hope it is a boy. I don't think I want any more sisters," Erik said with a sour face.

"Runa is a fine young lass," Ciarán said with a laugh.

Erik shook his head. "Nu uh. She is awful. She always cries when she doesn't get her way and Papa thinks it is my fault!"

Ciarán laughed. Runa was definitely her mother's

daughter with a matching strong will and a haughty exterior. She ruled the nursery, even going so far as to proclaim herself queen. When Erik had pointed out he would one day be King of Fadersogn, and she would marry someone far away, she'd burst into tears and ran off to find her father. The nanny tsked at him and ran off after the stricken three-year-old. Erik apologized when he caught up and told his side of the story to both of his parents, but Ciarán had not missed his defiant *but it was true*, spoken under his breath as he was returned to the nursery by the nanny. The boy would make a fine King one day. For her part, Runa was given a new doll and the matter was promptly forgotten.

"In time, you will both learn when it is appropriate to yield to the other and will become friends, for now, why don't we see to the new arrival?" Ciarán asked.

"Ok," the boy said, clinging tighter to Ciarán's neck as they made their way inside the castle.

Olav was just exiting when the two of them arrived in the corridor of the Queen's rooms. Ciarán gently let the boy down from his back and Erik ran to his father, jumping up and down with excitement.

"Papa, is it a boy? I hope it's a boy," he said, crossing his fingers behind his back for luck.

Olav smiled widely. "And if it were not, would you still love the child?"

Erik made a face. "I suppose, Papa. But is it?"

Olav nodded. "Indeed, my son. You have a new baby brother. Would you like to meet him?"

Erik clapped his little hands. "Oh yes please!"

Olav turned to let Erik into the room but his eyes met Ciarán's and he smiled tiredly.

"Captain Allyn, might you stay a moment so we may talk after I introduce my sons?" he asked.

Ciarán nodded. He waited in the corridor while the family got acquainted. He watched from the doorway as Erik peered at the baby in his father's arms. The baby cooed at Erik and then promptly sneezed in his face. The look on the boy's face was comical but Ciarán could tell that he was impressed by the tiny child. Olav asked one of the maids to return Erik to the nursery and they walked past Ciarán, Erik waving his goodbyes. Ciarán waved back and waited for Olav to return.

"Would you like to come in and see the baby?" Olav asked from the doorway.

Ciarán nodded and went into the room. He was startled to see Orla relaxing on a couch nearby. He had not known she was out of bed so early. Ciarán bowed to her and then took the seat Olav gestured to and sat next to him. Olav revealed the baby to Ciarán and he stared at it in wonder. It was so tiny and perfect.

"Would you like to hold him?" Orla asked.

Ciarán's head shot up and he shook his head.

"I'm not sure that is wise," he said, gesturing to his injured arm.

He had never held the other children when they were infants, too afraid he might drop them if they squirmed.

"Nonsense, here, rest your arm on the arm of the couch like this," Olav said, as he demonstrated what he meant.

Ciarán took up the position, resting his right arm against the couch. Olav placed the baby in Ciarán's arm, gently supporting the head in the crook of his elbow. Ciarán looked down at the little boy, longing to stroke the soft black hair he could see on the child's head. The baby opened his eyes, and Ciarán felt like he was looking in a mirror. Something dawned on him and he met Orla's eyes. She gave a little shrug and a secret smile. Their silent moment was interrupted by Olav.

"Ciarán, we would like to ask you a very serious question and much depends on your answer," he said sternly.

Ciarán swallowed hard, all his fears about Orla's reputation coming to stark reality. He was beginning to panic inside, ready to defend Orla at the expense of himself, when Olav's question registered in his brain.

"I'm sorry, what?" he asked, to make sure he had heard right.

"We would like you to be the godfather of our son, do you accept?" Olav asked again with an indulging smile.

Ciarán looked down at the baby. Godfather was a very big responsibility. He would be entrusted with the education of this young child in addition to his current duties. He would be a second father to the boy and it would fall to him to guide the child through life. He had no children of his own, could he do the job properly?

"Well?" Orla asked, nervous for his answer.

Ciarán gulped. "Aye," he said in a strangled voice. He cleared his throat. "It would be my honor, Your Majesties."

The baby was christened on a warm summer day as Ciarán proudly held him in his arm. The ceremony was as grand as those for Erik and Runa but this time Ciarán was a participant instead of an onlooker. He had practiced holding the child and walking with him countless times in the previous week. Orla had laughed at him, but he told her that this was the most important moment in his life. She'd understood and indulged him, patiently going through the ritual over and over again until he felt he had it down.

When it came time to name the child, Ciarán was brought to tears when Orla proudly pronounced to all that the child's name would be Quinn Lochlann. She looked at him, as if asking for permission, and he smiled gratefully and nodded his head almost imperceptibly. The crowd repeated the name and added *long may he live in peace and harmony,* and a great cheer arose, celebrating the infant and signaling the end of the ceremony.

Ciarán looked out from his seat of honor at the feast

and smiled at the crowd. He had never expected this kind of positive attention and it felt good for once to be able to receive it for something such as this, rather than the pity he usually got for his disability. The baby cooed from the bassinet and Ciarán reached out his hand, stroking Quinn's hair. He whispered to the child.

"Go to sleep little one, we have many adventures ahead of us and for that you must rest and grow strong."

Quinn grabbed Ciarán's finger with his tiny hand and squeezed. Ciarán smiled at the child and stroked his hand with his other fingers. Orla watched the pair of them with adoration plain for all to see. She was the happiest she had ever been in her entire life and she was pleased she could finally do something good to pay Ciarán back for all he had done for her.

chapter twelve

Ciarán's health continued to decline. He'd finally convinced Olav to make Orla stop sending in new remedies, they were killing him faster than the disease, each one more pungent and foul-tasting than the last. There was nothing that could truly be done anyways, it was now only a matter of time before he was gone. He wished to be left alone in peace, not prodded and studied as if he were a specimen under a glass jar.

On the days he felt well enough, he would sit at his writing desk and look to affairs that might need his attention. It was decided he would keep the estate and its income as gifted to him in recognition of his service to the kingdom but would continue living in his quarters at the castle. It was a compromise Olav suggested, and he readily agreed to in order to make Orla at least a little bit happier. It would mean he did not have to rely on Olav's generosity without being able to repay him for the kindness.

His ship was also still involved in commercial trading

and a new captain needed to be appointed. The previous captain had requested retirement and Ciarán was inclined to agree that it might be best. Olav helped interview a suitable replacement and Ciarán merely needed to complete the paperwork.

He worked as much as he could, the pain often preventing him from doing too much in one sitting. He stared out the window, losing track of time, the softly falling snow easing his mental burdens. It seemed the world was just more peaceful when it was covered in white. He'd never thought he would get used to living in such a cold kingdom but found it a pleasant distraction during his convalescence.

Orla asked him what he was doing and he merely told her he was ensuring the future. She laughed bitterly at that statement and told him it seemed there would be no future. He yearned to soothe her misery but knew this was the one thing he could not fix for her.

Olav visited on several occasions and they talked, Ciarán relaying the things he hoped would happen upon his death. They both tried to find a way to help Orla after his passing. Olav had seen what happened with Phelan and Meara and he desperately wanted to spare Orla that fate. Ciarán assured him this was different, and although he agreed, he silently believed that it was, indeed, no different. Orla loved Ciarán more than anyone else in the world and his death would devastate her.

The season changed into spring and the first flowers began to bloom. Ciarán had a minor reprieve from the illness with the warmer air and once again Orla's spirits lifted. Runa tried to talk reason into her mother, but Orla would have none of it. Surely this would be the time that Ciarán beat the illness and she would be spared the pain of his death. He had never let her down and this would be no different. No one could convince her otherwise and it pained them all to see that she would not listen to reason. She allowed the children to see him again, after he practically begged her to relent, and all three of them spent as much time as they could, knowing this was the end.

A late winter storm hit the kingdom, killing the newly sprung flowers and freezing the entire countryside with a thick layer of ice. Ciarán's coughing returned with a vengeance, he was barely able to speak at times because of it. Orla's newfound happiness was frozen along with everything else. She locked herself in her rooms and refused to listen to anyone who might speak with her about Captain Allyn. She did not visit him, for fear that if she did, she would have to recognize the inevitable. She did not want to say goodbye.

Three days after the frost hit, Orla was awoken from her pre-dinner nap by one of her maids. The physician was standing in her sitting rooms and her heart plummeted to her stomach. After he assured her the Captain was still alive but not likely to survive the night, she rushed to Ciarán's rooms, taking only a moment to wrap a dressing gown around her nightdress. Once there, she sent the physician and everyone else away. She took a deep shuddering breath and then went into the room.

"Hey beautiful." Ciarán smiled.

It was rare for him to be so informal and it caught Orla off guard. He must definitely be dying to throw such caution to the wind. She hesitated for a moment and Ciarán began coughing violently, his entire body shaking in the process.

Orla rushed to his side and gasped at the sight of the blood soaking his handkerchief. She went to the basin and grabbed a warm, wet cloth. She gently wiped his lips and helped lay him back against the pillows that had been propped up for comfort.

"You've been keeping things from me. I have never seen the blood," she admonished.

He nodded. "I did not want you to worry."

"I have worried since the first moment you returned from Eiremor with this cough," she said.

"Aye, but this was too much for you to handle."

"Oh Ciarán," Orla said and a tear fell down her face.

"It's all right, darling," he said.

She shook her head. Then she removed her dressing gown and lifted the comforter.

"What are you doing?" he asked.

She lifted his arm and put it around her, then placed her cheek on his chest. "Shh, Ciarán.... can we just for once forget about the rest for tonight? Just for tonight can we be together? I know I asked you this once before and I promised it would never happen again but please just indulge me this one last time. You are just Ciarán and I am just Orla and we are where we belong, together."

"What will the servants say? They will gossip and it will get back to Olav. This will hurt him."

"I have sent them away for the evening, they are not to disturb you until I say they may return. Olav and I talked about this moment. I didn't want to but he made me listen. He knew more than I what I needed. He told me about Lochlann long ago and he understands. Please, Ciarán?" she pleaded with him.

"Aye, my love, if you are sure," Ciarán relented and pulled her closer, dropping a kiss on her head.

Orla started to cry. "I need more time."

"I know, Orla. I have tried to be strong and give you more. I'm sorry I have failed you," he said.

She shook her head. "You never failed me. It is I who failed you. I should have waited for you, no matter how long. I should have known you would not leave me. I could have made them wait but my mother convinced me to let you go. I gave up on you too soon and ruined everything."

She was sobbing uncontrollably now. Ciarán held her

while she sobbed, rubbing her arm and holding her close.

"Orla, I don't blame you. How could I? You have always been perfect in my eyes. A little stubborn at times and definitely strong-willed, but you allowed me to be near you and that was a balm to my heart. You gave me a life I never thought possible." He was now unable to hold back his own tears.

"It wasn't enough," she whispered.

His arm tightened around her and he swallowed a lump in his throat. "You were always enough. Just being in the same room was enough. I should have told you when I left, even though you didn't want me to do so. I never told you when I returned, it would have been selfish of me. I have always loved you. You are my heart and it is yours."

"I love you Ciarán. It was always you. I didn't understand it, and I fought it, but it was always you," she said.

"Aye, I knew. I didn't need you to say the words. It took me a long time to realize it, but I knew."

Orla reached up and kissed him softly. It was a kiss filled with lost love and longing. Shortly his coughing grew worse once again and she helped him through the episode. When he lay back, exhausted, she looked up at his still handsome face and eyes filled with pain.

"Would you like for me to help you feel better?" she asked.

"That would be brilliant, love" he replied through a grimace.

Orla raised her hands over his heart.

"Wait, will it knock me out?" he asked. "I don't want to miss the time I have left with you."

She shook her head. "No, it will only mask the pain for awhile, I promise."

He smiled and she proceeded to cast the spell. He had not let her use her magic on him before, for fear that it would give her false hope. He relaxed in relief as each breath got easier until it almost felt as if he was not sick at all. The calm before the storm, he thought, the sea still in his blood after all these years.

"Thank you, my love," he said when she was finished.

They talked for hours and Orla could tell that the exhaustion was creeping up on him. His words were starting to get a little slurred and he was having trouble keeping his eyes open. He had not slept well in weeks due to the coughing and she knew that she should let him rest, but was reluctant to let him do so.

"I think you need to sleep now," she told him.

"Aye, but I don't want this to end. I'm not afraid, only worried about what will happen to you when I am gone. I swore to protect you, forever," he said.

Orla choked back another sob as a tear rolled down her cheek. "Rest now, and I will be here when you wake."

Ciarán looked at her. "Orla, I love you."

"I love you as well. Rest," she said and laid down beside him, held in his arm. He was just drifting off when she decided to tell him one last thing.

"Ciarán?"

"Hmm?" he hummed sleepily.

"Quinn... he's, well he is..." Orla was struggling with how to tell him.

Ciarán gave a small chuckle. "I know."

She raised up to look at him. "You do?"

"Aye... his eyes give him away. He is the product of true love. Take care of him for me?" he asked.

Orla nodded and kissed him again.

"One thing that puzzled me, you gave him my brother's name?" Ciarán asked.

Orla nodded and stroked his cheek. "Olav loved your brother dearly, he was his best friend and could have been so much more if not for the mistakes Olav and I made. We both agreed Ciarán would be too conspicuous and draw unwanted comparisons. We wanted Quinn to have some small part of his heritage, even if he did not know it. I promise I will tell him when he is older."

Ciarán's eyes widened. "Olav knew?"

"About everything, the night in Eiremor after my father's death and when I knew I was pregnant. The pregnancy was very different but I, too, am able to protect the ones I love. We kept the confirmation of Quinn's true parentage from you so that you could honestly deny it if asked. You are often too honorable for your own good and would have been unable to lie. We gave you as much access to him as we could by making you his godfather," she replied honestly.

"Thank you, I was truly honored and he lessened the pain of my brother's passing. Thank you for allowing me to be a part of all your children's lives. They are a testament to their mother."

Orla smile and nodded, unable to speak around the lump in her throat. She lay back down in his arms and listened to his breathing even out into sleep.

Orla did not sleep as she held the man she had loved for so long in her arms for the last time. She wanted him to be at peace even as part of her wanted him to fight like hell. He had always fought for her and it was time she let him rest. She had to let him go. Sometime in the early morning, she could feel his breathing getting shallower. Frown lines appeared and she soothed them away.

"Shh, my love, it is okay. You deserve to rest now. I love you," she said as she kissed his forehead, then his lips.

He croaked out, "Be strong, my love. I will wait for you."

She rested her head over his heart as he breathed his last. She sobbed for their fate and for the man who had deserved so much more. She sobbed for herself and all that she had lost because of her stubbornness and her pride. Finally, she sobbed for their child, who would never again get to speak to the man he had only known as his uncle. A good man, too honorable to decry the fate he had been dealt. Finally, when she had no tears left, she composed herself and called for help.

ETERNAL WILLOW

On a quiet spring day, the King and Queen and their children attended a small ceremony at a manor house in the country. Their beloved friend and Uncle, was laid out on a funeral pyre built naturally by the stream. The Queen had helped prepare the body and, unbeknownst to anyone else, had placed a beautiful ammolite pendant in his hand. The very same pendant he had gifted the Princess of Eiremor, *on the auspicious occasion of her birth, if belated by unimaginable circumstances.* The one the Queen had worn every day since she had received it from her very best friend.

The family stood there, saying their goodbyes, each telling the others a happy memory of the Captain.

"Ciarán Allyn was the most noble man I had the pleasure of knowing. Once, he and I were on a mission to help our neighbors to the south deal with an invasion. I never told any of you this." Olav's eyes met Orla's. "But we were attacked by brigands and surrounded. He fought well and protected me from a near fatal blow at the expense of injuring his own arm. We were able to defeat the attackers, and when we were back at the castle, while the medics were stitching him up, he said to me *let's keep this between us, if you will, Your Majesty. No need to make a fuss over something that didn't happen.* He didn't want you to worry about his safety and he did not want to make me look weak. He was a truly honorable man and I will miss him."

Olav laid a flower at Ciarán's shrouded feet. Erik spoke next.

"Uncle Ciarán used to give me piggyback rides and teach me sword fighting. He was my best friend for so long. He knew what I was thinking before I would even speak and his council meant so much to me. He has taught me what it means to be selfless."

Erik laid another flower at Ciarán's feet and squeezed his sister's hand. She shook her head but he whispered encouragement in her ear and she took a steadying breath.

"I was always a spoiled brat," she said.

Everyone laughed and Orla looked at her daughter fondly. Runa shrugged.

"Well, it's true. Uncle Ciarán didn't let that stop him from making sure I always saw the error in my ways. He never squashed my spirit; he let me be free, but he was firm in his lessons. I never quite knew I was learning something until later reflection, but then the genius of what he said would register, and I would understand why he had spoken in such a way. He knew how to make me see things without forcing me to see them."

Runa broke off into a sob and buried her face in Orla's chest. She sobbed and Orla rubbed her back. After a moment, she straightened and solemnly laid her flower at the end of Ciarán's feet. She stared off into the water, refusing to look at her family or the pyre. Uncle Ciarán had understood her like no one else had.

They all looked at Quinn, waiting patiently for him to acknowledge them. He had refused to speak with anyone since Ciarán died, and only reluctantly came with them to this ceremony. He was like a lost puppy, as if his soul was shattered by the loss of his godfather. He sniffled and looked at the pyre. He walked up to it and laid a hand where Ciarán's lay underneath the cloth. He looked up at his mother.

"Mother?" he asked in a quiet voice.

Orla went over to her son and put her hands on his shoulders.

Quinn whispered, "I don't have just one happy memory. They were all happy."

Orla's tears started anew and she hugged her son. He clung to her and she could feel the buzzing along his skin from the magic that was barely contained.

"Would you like to tell him something?" she asked.

"Could I do it without the others hearing?" he pleaded.

Orla nodded. His father and siblings walked a little distance away and Quinn grabbed his mother's hand.

"Don't go too far," he said with some fear.

"I will be here within reach, my little love," she said.

Quinn nodded. He walked up to the head of the pyre and put his hands on either side of Ciarán's head.

"Father," he whispered. "I know why you could not tell me when I asked but I know in my heart you are my father. I'm not ready for you to be gone but I will remember my promise. I will find my true love and I will never let her go, you have my word as a gentleman and as your son. I will make you proud of me."

Quinn laid a tiny miniature portrait of himself next to Ciarán on the pyre and stepped back. Orla did her best to act like she had not overheard his words but he knew she had. Orla hugged her son, fiercely holding him to her, the last part of Ciarán she had left. Quinn squeezed her back and then extracted himself and ran back to the manor, not wanting them to see his tears. He was too old to cry, he wasn't a baby anymore. The others rejoined Orla.

Olav cleared his throat. "Orla? Would you like to say something?"

"Captain Allyn... Ciarán was my best friend. He... he..." She found she could not continue.

Olav wanted to give Orla the last moments alone with her lost love. He looked toward his children.

"Erik, Runa, let's go back to the manor."

They nodded and followed their father back to the house. Runa looked back at her mother standing next to the pyre as if frozen in time.

"Papa, will Mother be all right?" she asked, wringing her hands.

Olav looked back at Orla and shook his head. "I don't know, Runa. The best we can do is be there for her during this difficult time. She has lost something very rare."

Orla stood next to the pyre and stared at Ciarán's face

through the cloth. His handsome face, lost to her forever. She would never again see his eyes or the way he looked at her. She would never watch his eyebrow raise in mischief or hear his laughter. She would never be comforted by him, the only person who could calm her down when she was irritated and unable to see clearly. She would never argue with him again. So many nevers lining up to be remembered.

"It is not fair, you must wait for me yet again, but I hope you do. I will look for you in the next life, my love."

She bent over him and placed a kiss against his lips. She stepped back taking a steadying breath. She thought of all the happy moments they had shared. The time he stood in the upper hall for hours, waiting for her to appear, just so he could shower her with flowers the moment she passed under the balcony. Or when he would sneak down to the kitchens and nab a loaf of fresh-baked bread before the cook could catch him when she mentioned how good it smelled. Little things he had always done in an attempt to make her smile or brighten her day.

A bright white fireball formed in her hands, and she released it, setting the pyre aflame. Orla stood there crying silently until the very last flame extinguished and the sun sank behind the mountains, leaving the sky in oranges and pinks. Quinn watched from the window, his hand against the pane of glass. If he placed it just so, he could only see the colors the pyre made and pretend it was the sunlight dancing off the clouds.

Ciarán left all his worldly possessions to Orla and her children, though they were far less than Orla realized. He had truly led a life of an eternal servant. Erik was given his compass, so that he may follow the true path of a great king, and Lochlann's sextant, so he may find his way even in the darkest of nights. Ciarán explained in a letter to Erik that out of all the children, Erik would gain the most and he hoped the future King would forgive the meager gift. Erik had swiped angrily at a tear that leaked out and told his family that his were the most cherished gifts of all of them. He gave them places of honor in his rooms and made sure they were kept polished for the rest of his life, to be passed down to his eldest son upon his death.

Princess Runa was given the maps Ciarán had hand drawn of all the places he had been so she might find her way wherever she roamed. He had even declared one unnamed island, *Runa's Escape*. He also gave her the commission to *The Return* with instructions that no matter where she went, she should always remember home and return there whenever possible. He reminded her that home is a place that never forgets who you are and always welcomes you back. He advised her that her family was the most precious gift she would ever be given. Runa committed those maps to memory and added to them, eventually publishing a world atlas and dispersing it for free to all the kingdoms she visited.

Quinn was given the deed to the manor house estate. Ciarán acknowledged that as a second son, Quinn might want a place of his own, not underneath the feet of his brother. Quinn stuck his tongue out at Erik when that part was read aloud and it earned him a hair tussle from Erik. The brothers laughed, for even though there was an age difference, they had always been close. It helped bring some levity to the otherwise solemn proceedings. Quinn was also bequeathed the remainder of Ciarán's possessions, save a small chest that was to be given to Her Majesty. As a final reminder, Ciarán instructed Quinn to follow his heart wherever it may lead and trust that it knew best. Quinn eventually filled the manor house with several magical children and it became a place of laughter and joy.

Finally, Orla was alone in her rooms with what Ciarán

had left her. It was a small chest that she had yet to open for fear of its contents. She had not wanted to explore it in front of her family because she felt odd having them watch her while she looked at what Ciarán thought important enough to leave her. She ran her hands along the top, lovingly circling the elaborate C engraved in the top. Ciarán had never bought flashy things and the engraving was the most expensive thing on the otherwise plain chest. She smiled at his frugality.

She opened the chest and her breath hitched in her throat. Inside the lid, "OC" was engraved in the same style as the C on the outside, hidden for all but Ciarán's eyes. She began looking through the contents.

First, there was a small bundle of dried forget-me-nots. It had always been her favorite flower. They'd picked them endlessly when they were teenagers, Ciarán adorning her head in a crown of them and pronouncing her the loveliest of all maidens in the meadow. She wondered when he did this and how long he'd kept them. They were still as purple-blue as when they were fresh and they had a smell of magic about them. She smiled; Kellan must have helped Ciarán preserve them.

Another piece of parchment held an etching of the willow tree back in Eiremor. It was their initials, intertwined, which Ciarán had carved into the tree one day during their courtship. He'd apologized to the tree when the wind made it creak and told it that it could be a witness at their wedding. Orla laughed and asked him what made him so sure she would marry him. He had merely shrugged and scratched behind his ear, focusing on his carving. There was a small branch from the tree with the long green leaves still attached. That tree had always been Ciarán's favorite thinking spot.

The next item was Lochlann's Medal of Honor from the War. Ciarán had treasured that medal and kept it with him every day after his brother passed. Orla did not remember it missing at Lochlann's funeral, but she had been so worried about her own father, she had also failed to comfort Ciarán at the time. She shook her head sadly at the wasted moments.

Finally, there was a note tied with a bright, blue ribbon, the exact color of his and Quinn's eyes. A lump was in the middle of the ribbon where only the knot should be.

Orla unfurled the ribbon and a ring fell into her hands. It was a beautiful silver band with a small ammolite stone set into it. A perfect match for the pendant he had given her for her birthday so long ago. It must have cost him a great deal of money. Orla examined it in the candlelight and found that inside the band was engraved the words, "To the end of time." She removed her wedding band and placed the new ring on her finger. It fit perfectly.

Orla read the note and covered a sob while tears streamed down her face once again, dropping onto the parchment:

My dearest love,

Our time is growing short and I do not know how to say everything that I must. I fear I have not served you faithfully. It was my duty to be your guard and I have carried out those duties as best I could these many years. I realize that as my Queen, you are the only one who has the power to release me from my position but I am afraid, darling, that the God of Death has other plans.

The only important thing is to tell you I love you. Nothing else matters but those words.

Death will not change my love for you and I will love you even beyond its icy grasp, until the universe blinks out of existence and the sky is blackened forever. You are my heart and I would only wish that you protect it and carry on. Please don't argue with me, Orla, as I know you must be doing so at this moment. Let us not fight.

Your children need their Mother to be strong and brave and I have every faith you will see them grow into wonderful and benevolent rulers, adventurers, and magicians. Encourage them to be the best version of themselves and they will not let you down.

Many years ago I was prepared to give you this ring and swear my life to you forever. The war came and you asked me to wait and I did. I had every intention of sweeping you off your feet with my military victories. Alas, I was too late and another came and took you away. I do not blame you for this and, in truth, you had my oath of forever even without the ring. I give it to you now as a token of my undying devotion, for *even in death I am still yours. Thank you for everything, my one true love. Until we meet again, my heart.*

Yours to the end of the world or time or both,

Ciarán

Kellan accepted the messenger from Fadersogn with a heavy heart. The messenger relayed the death of his beloved friend and delivered a package from His Majesty of Fadersogn, Olav. Kellan read the note from Olav and dismissed the messenger for refreshments and rest before he returned to his kingdom. Kellan's wife squeezed his hand with sympathy and excused herself and the rest of the courtiers.

Kellan made his way through the meadow and down to the willow tree by the river. He sat kneeling down next to a memorial for Lochlann and smiled. Ciarán had timidly asked if he could place it here in honor of his brother and Kellan had wholeheartedly given his approval. Lochlann had been like a big brother to him. Kellan removed a stubborn weed growing next to the memorial.

"Lochlann, my friend, it seems that your brother has come home. Our generation is slowly making way for the new," he said to himself.

Kellan looked around, deciding the best place for Ciarán's remains. Olav had gone to great lengths to ensure that Ciarán's wishes regarding his final resting place were personally overseen by himself. Orla had insisted on a memorial plaque in the temple and Olav granted that request as well, without argument. In private, he convinced his wife that Ciarán missed Eiremor and wished to be in his favorite place. She had nodded and bit her lip, fearing to be so far away from what remained of him, but understanding that it might be best. He would want the serenity of his willow tree.

Kellan spotted the carving on the tree and smiled to himself. He used his magic to open a door in the tree and placed the ashes within, sealing it again so that no one would be wise to its hidden contents. He placed a hand on the tree and closed his eyes.

"Look after him well," he said quietly and returned to the castle. The breeze rustled the leaves of the tree and it creaked quietly as if in agreement, welcoming Ciarán home.

epilogue
ten years later

Orla sat in her garden, soaking up the last sun of fall before winter hit and she would be forced indoors. Her King and husband, Olav, had fallen from a horse just a year after Ciarán's death and taken ill from the wound. The physicians did all they could, but in the end, the wound was too great, and the King too tired. Orla mourned him for many months, as he had been a devoted husband and father and she had loved him. She had lost the two men she cared for most in the world in a short time, and it almost broke her but she carried on for her children. Now her children had grown into young adults with lives of their own and she was alone more often than not.

Runa had taken up the rank of Captain on *The Return* after much cajoling with Erik and an agreement that she would keep a bodyguard on the ship and stay away from known pirate-infested waters. Her brother always had a hard time denying her when she pouted and this was no exception. She spoke to Orla about what her Uncle Ciarán had told her, reminding Orla of her own desires for adventure when she had been young, and Orla had backed her up. Ciarán had prepared the crew for this eventuality, and they were enamored with their new Captain. Each man would protect her to a fault. She wrote often of the places she saw and kept journals of everything she did. Orla wondered if her daughter would ever settle down, she was such a restless spirit. She envied her daughter the freedom she had, but kept it to herself.

Quinn was still learning his magic, refining it to aid others. He wanted to become a healer and find a cure for the illnesses that had taken both of his fathers. During a journey to Noregfjord, he met Britt, another healer—one without magic—who was also intent on making the world a better place. She had grand ideas of curing basic illnesses using plants found in the countryside of her home. Quinn felt sparks the first moment he met her. He was drawn to her. She feared she was not good enough for him, since she was of low birth, but Quinn assured her that in his eyes, she was perfect. He had recently written to his mother and brother asking if he might bring his new love home to Fadersogn. He wanted to marry her and work with her on their shared passion of the healing arts. Both agreed and Orla would be happy to be reunited with her youngest son and meet his fiancé.

Erik had become the beloved King that Ciarán had predicted. His reign was peaceful and the people flourished under his reforms. He instituted improved methods of food storage for the winter and an educational institute that welcomed both girls and boys. Many of the young women in the institute were graduating at the heads of their classes. Soon, he would be welcoming one exceptionally talented young woman to join his council of advisors. It would be the first time a woman had served in that official capacity.

Orla smiled at all her children had accomplished in

such a short time. They were smart, talented, and delightful conversationalists. She and Olav had taught them well but she also gave Ciarán the credit he was due. She did not think her children would have been as successful without his guidance. She could not be more proud of them but she recognized she was no longer needed. She had done her job and it was time to let them be in the light. She should retire to the shadows. She got up from her chair and went inside to dress for dinner.

That evening, the beloved Dowager Queen, Orla of Fadersogn passed quietly in the night. She had not been particularly ill and had only retired the night before claiming she was just a little more tired that day than usual. King Erik held a state funeral for his mother and the country mourned their beloved Queen. Erik had an elaborate tomb built next to his father's, complete with an effigy in the likeness of the Queen, reposing as if just asleep. For hundreds of years after, the tomb would be covered in flowers in remembrance of the Queen, who had saved them in the Great War.

After the mourners had all departed to return to their normal lives, the Queen's children stood next to a funeral pyre in the exact spot where Ciarán's had been. Runa cried on her brother's shoulder while Quinn held Britt's hand. They each looked at their mother for the last time and remembered when she had been there with them for this ceremony for another lost loved one.

After a moment, Erik nodded his head at Quinn. Quinn spoke softly to his fiancé and moved in front of his siblings. He lit a white fireball in his hand and placed it on the pyre, setting it aflame. As the flames expanded, they could just make out the outline of their mother under her funeral shroud. She had a wreath of forget-me-nots in her hair, which Runa had lovingly braided, and on her left hand she wore the silver wedding band she'd never worn in life. Quinn added it just before she was wrapped in her shroud. He'd found it, and the letter from Ciarán, when he and

Runa were looking through their mother's things. He felt it was right and his Papa would understand. Just before Olav died, he had whispered instructions to Quinn, and Quinn was a man of his word, just like his true father.

The four adults watched the fire burn, then Erik led Runa and Britt back to the manor. In a gesture reminiscent of his mother's so many years ago, Quinn remained and watched until the pyre burned its last and the sun had long left the sky. He had grown up so much since the day of Ciarán's funeral and he could now face the future, knowing his mother would want him to be happy. Later, he would place a stone bench in this spot that had seen so much sorrow, surrounded by forget-me-nots that magically never died, even in the dead of winter. His everlasting tribute to his parents.

Quinn met his uncle Kellan by the willow tree. Both men had cried together, Quinn for his mother and Kellan for his sister. They had found solace in the shared grief.

Kellan had been happy to meet Britt, she was a fine match for his youngest nephew and very well-spoken. He listened to their plans for healing the sick with enthusiasm and pledged his help if they should need it. His only sorrow, meeting his nephew's fiancé, was that his sister had not gotten the chance to see how happy she made her son.

Now, their final act before Quinn returned home was to lay Orla to rest.

"Olav was a wise man, I never gave him enough credit for that," Kellan said.

"Aye, Papa knew that mother would never ask him for this but he wanted to do what was right. He loved mother and he understood her so well. He told me they had been separated long enough," Quinn agreed.

Kellan nodded. He opened the door in the tree with his magic and pulled out the vase holding Ciarán's ashes. He opened the vase and held it steady for Quinn. Quinn poured the ashes of his mother into the vase and then reached into his pocket. He pulled out the ring, which had magically not burned in the funeral pyre. He placed it on top of the ashes and Kellan replaced the lid.

"Uncle Kellan, before we replace it in the tree, would you perform a marriage ceremony?" Quinn asked.

Kellan's eyes widened but he thought a moment and nodded. He said the words of Eiremor's traditional marriage ceremony and blessed the vase. Then he replaced the lid and Quinn set it gently back into the tree, caressing it as he did so.

Kellan used his magic to seal the hiding spot once more. He placed a hand on Quinn's shoulder then headed back to the castle, leaving the young man to say his final goodbyes to his parents alone. Quinn placed his hand on the tree over the intertwining "OC" and performed a spell of his own. The tree glowed and the "OC" became a silvery green, a permanent memorial to his parents.

"Father, I have kept my word and found my true love. I will hold onto her and treasure her for the rest of my life. So, now you can be together with mother for eternity. Uncle Kellan has married you in death, which you were denied in life. May you have the happiness that eluded you when you were alive."

Quinn kissed his fingers and laid them against the tree, silently thanking it for being their final resting place. He walked back towards the castle, watching the stars twinkling overhead. Later he would tell his wife and children that he swore two stars shone brighter in the sky that night.